Published by Oliver-Heber Books

0 9 8 7 6 5 4 3 2 1

TOWN OF ILLUSIONS

A.N. SAGE

OLIVERHEBERBOOKS

CONTENTS

Chapter One

Billie

"Who's Morgan?" Peyton's words tore through me, slicing my heart like sharpened daggers.

I had only been back from the retched entrapment of the cavern for a day and already, trouble had caught up with me. Somehow, Shadowhurst would not let me breathe easy. Looking around at my friends gathered in Peyton's backyard, I could almost taste their confusion at my question, and it made me nervous to speak again. There was no way none of them remembered Morgan. It simply wasn't possible. People didn't vanish into thin air, and even if they did, they were not so easily forgotten.

Of course, this was Shadowhurst, and stranger things have happened. Granted, usually, those strange things involved the High Coven I was apparently at war with after my betrayal of siding with the shadowers. Though none of that was my fault. The shadowers were innocent bystanders and a product of the coven's evil dealings with magic. Not that any of that mattered to the witches I used to think of as family. They hated the shadowers almost as much as they hated me. At least as much as I *assumed* they hated me these days.

Witches didn't disobey the High Coven. They just didn't.

Until me.

Behind me, River's chest rose and fell against my back, offering a small amount of solitude in the darkness creeping over my mind. I still couldn't believe no one here remembered Morgan, but mostly, I couldn't believe Peyton didn't. From what River told me, those two had grown quite close since I was gone.

I laughed under my breath at the thought. Gone was a funny way of describing what I'd been through the last week. And ,as it turned out, I was about to go through a hell of a lot more.

My eyes scanned the yard again, then landed back on Peyton. "Guys, come on," I urged my friends. "You're joking, right?"

"Babe," River whispered against my neck. "You sure you're feeling okay?"

Definitely not. Not by a long shot.

The sun rose above us, spreading its golden rays over the yard and casting sharp shadows on my friends' faces. From this angle, the bunch of them resembled sinister characters from a campfire ghost story, though I knew that was only my imagination running away with me again. These people were my friends, my family, and whatever was going on, there had to be a reason for this.

They were playing a trick on me. That had to be it.

"River," I said, forcing a smile, "you're not serious. Where is she? Are you guys setting me up?" I pulled out of

River's embrace and looked around the yard. "Morgan! You can come out now! Joke's over!"

Everything was so quiet that I could hear the light rustle of water in Peyton's pool when the wind picked up. My eyes darted around the empty backyard, counting to ten in my head to give Morgan a chance to jump out of the bushes and scare me. *These tools better have a good explanation for doing this the first time they see me after that cavern garbage. Not cool.*

When Morgan remained out of sight, I crossed my arms and turned to River. "This isn't funny anymore."

"B, no one knows what you're talking about," Peyton said, concern coating every word. "Maybe this was a bad idea, getting you out here. You should probably get some rest, girl. We can all catch up tomorrow at school."

"She's right." River nodded. "Come on, I'll take you home."

"I'm not going anywhere until you all stop acting like weirdos and tell me why Morgan isn't here. Did something happen? Did she get hurt?"

Across the table from where we stood, Savannah and Logan exchanged shrugs. Their faces grew ashen before me, and I fought the urge to snap at them to speak their minds. At least I attempted to. Before I could stop myself, I was crossing the distance between us and shoving my face right in Savannah's. "You two know something. Spill it," I hissed.

"Look," Savannah said, unimpressed. "I get you've been through some shit, but you best take a step back before we have a problem. Listen to your boyfriend and go home. Relax. And stop spewing crazy crap. It's weird AF."

My jaw clenched and I balled my fists, ready to take her down, when fingers wrapped around my wrist. I swirled to see Ms. Broussard's narrowed eyes on mine, her shoulders rising to touch her ears.

"Billie, dear," the shop owner said sweetly. "You've been through a lot, and we all understand the toll exhaustion can take on someone's body. Your friends are right, you need your rest. There is nothing like a good sleep to cure a clouded mind."

"My mind isn't clouded," I ground out. "If you guys wanted to mess with me, today is not a good day for that. It's tacky."

"Drama queen..." Savannah breathed out, earning herself a well-directed death glare.

I peeled my gaze from her and studied the rest of the people in the yard. Behind Savannah and Logan, Raiden wrapped an arm around Mel to pull her into him. Worry settled in the creases of both their brows and the two shifter leaders stared at me, unblinking. It was eerie, to say the least and I had to look down at my boots, suddenly finding my shoelaces to be extremely interesting. When I could no longer feel their heated eyes on me, I dared to glance at the remaining three witch hunters in the group. Abigail was as disinterested in my outbursts as she normally was, occupying herself with petting Tyler's chest instead. Beside them, Jayden opened and closed his mouth like he was trying to think of something funny to say. Luckily for all of us, he kept his thoughts to himself, choosing to run his fingers through his hair while watching me. His dark eyes scanned my face in the same manner I assumed shrinks used when they were trying to rate your level of crazy on a scale of one to ten. Judging by his expression, I was falling close to a solid forty-five and it made me all that much more confused.

What if this wasn't some trick? What if they actually didn't remember Morgan?

My head pounded and my mouth dried as the realization hit me. If I was the only one who knew Morgan existed, we were in deep shit. Something was going on and I had no idea what it was. I hated not knowing. It was a fate worse than death as far as I was concerned.

Slowly, River came to stand next to me and the woodsy scent of his cologne invaded my senses. His green eyes deepened in shade as he searched my face before pressing a palm to my cheek. "Babe..." he whispered, running a finger across my chin. "Let's just get you home and we'll figure all this out later."

"I'm not crazy," I snapped and shook him off. "I know what I remember."

"No one is saying you're crazy, but you've gone through Hell. It would make sense your mind is all over the place right now. Maybe this is just a by-product of what happened to you in that cave."

Could he be right? I didn't want to believe it, but my time in the cavern did mess me up real good, and there was no telling what else happened while I was there. I mean, I made up Naomi, so who's to say I wasn't doing the same thing with Morgan? There was little we knew about the fae magic I experienced while I was imprisoned in that damn place. Maybe this was part of it.

Squaring my shoulders, I turned to Vic, the only other witch in our messed up group of friends.

"Can fae magic do this? Make me remember someone that never existed?" I asked.

Vic's brow scrunched and she shrugged. "No clue. But I'll look into it."

"Thanks," I said. "This doesn't make any sense! For sure, no one is messing with me here?"

They shook their heads in unison, making me feel even more insane than I already was. This wasn't a trick my friends were playing, and if it was, they deserved to win awards for their performance. Still, I wouldn't peg them to do something like this. There was no point to it. They were my family, and family didn't make someone feel batshit crazy for no reason. Something was wrong inside my brain, something that was making me remember Morgan as though she truly existed. This couldn't be good.

And I'm officially going insane. Wonderful.

Whatever happened to me left a mark, one that was threatening to shatter my reality, and I dreaded every second of it. Inside, magic slithered against my skin, and I stifled it back down. The last thing I wanted was to lose control in front of everyone. It was bad enough I was acting like a lunatic, they didn't need to see my magic explode on top of it. Whether or not Morgan was real, I couldn't break apart right now. At least not completely.

Keeping my act together was the only way to get through this, and while I still didn't completely believe I made Morgan up, I was willing to give my friends the benefit of the doubt.

The cavern showed me so many lies, and I believed each one at my weakest point. Morgan could be nothing more than a figment of my imagination. One that seemed so real, I couldn't wrap my mind around any other option.

Either that or I was certifiable, and I wasn't willing to accept that yet.

I wasn't nuts. I was just coping.

Turning on my heels, I faced Peyton. "Meet you in the parking lot before first period tomorrow?"

"You bet your ass, B!" She beamed up at me. "I'll bring the snacks, you bring the coffees. Some of those fancy ones Thomas makes with the cinnamon sprinkles."

"How come we don't get coffees?" Savannah asked with a smirk.

"Keep the 'tude in check and we might consider it."

Peyton winked, and I struggled to smile against my better judgment.

Heart still pounding, I entwined my fingers in River's and leaned into him. His warm breath fanned my face and I let my shoulders sag as I pushed the panic away. Whatever was happening to me wasn't ideal, but I couldn't let the cavern win. I patted the small stone in my pocket, a staurolite as it turned out, and thought of Naomi, the imaginary friend I made in that prison. All I had left of her was the stone, and I carried it with me everywhere as a reminder to keep my head clear and my emotions in check. Maybe I could find another knick knack to do the same with Morgan. An item to keep me grounded while I attempted to have a normal life yet again. Thinking of Morgan threw me for a loop, and I searched the backyard again for a girl I wasn't even sure was real. My body tensed and sweat pooled at the base of my neck while I tried to collect myself. Near to me, River's brow furrowed as he looked me over, worry settling in every corner of his eyes.

Great. One day back and I already had a massive headache and two imaginary friends. *Way to go, Billie. Awesome way to cope with the shitstorm your life has become. Just freaking stellar.*

Chapter Two

River

*P*ulling into Billie's driveway, I tried to keep my eyes straight ahead to avoid looking at her every few seconds, which was what I had been doing the entire time we drove to her place. Worry spread through me each time I watched her turn to stare absently out the window, biting her lower lip nervously. Vic and Ms. Broussard warned me that the traumatic experience Billie had gone through could influence her, but this was not what any of us were expecting. Making up a person? Stable people didn't do that, and her insistence at Peyton's place that this Morgan person existed stressed me the hell out.

It made my wolf go bonkers too, which wasn't helping one bit.

Simmer down, moron.

I put the car in park and peeled my hands off the steering wheel, realizing how tightly I've been clutching it for the first time. One look at Billie had me twisted up inside and I couldn't bear seeing her go through this alone.

But how could I help her? I did not understand what was

happening or why she made up an entire human being. This was way out of my wheelhouse. Out of all of ours, really.

"How are you doing?" I asked, feeling like an idiot immediately. *How do you think she's doing?*

Billie glanced at me briefly, then turned to the window again. Her blue eyes went milky, and her lips parted as she took a deep breath in. Everything about her seemed broken and it tore me up. Carefully, I reached for her hand, relieved when she didn't pull away.

"I know you're scared, but no one is saying you're making this up," I said when she still didn't answer me. "We're just worried."

Seriously, dude, just stop talking. Stop. Right. Now.

Billie's face scrunched and she resumed chewing on her bottom lip. "I'm not scared," she finally uttered, providing me with no relief at all. "I think I'm going crazy."

"Babe, don't say that. You said it yourself, this is probably the cave's effect on you. We'll figure it out, I promise."

"And if it's not?" she asked. "You really don't remember her, do you?"

I had no idea how to answer her question. On the one hand, whoever this Morgan was, she wasn't real, and I desperately wanted to tell her that. On the other, Billie was always rational and headstrong, so I knew there was more to this than just the aftermath of trauma. Something was going on in her head that I knew nothing about, and I hated not being able to help her get through it. I was so useless, it hurt my head just thinking about it.

Tracing my thumb against her soft skin, I unbuckled and scooted closer to the passenger side of the car. The fresh peony smell of her shampoo lingered in the air, and I closed my eyes to breathe her in. After everything we went through,

Billie was finally back. She was sitting right next to me, and yet, she was miles away. It was as though only a part of her came back while another stayed in that cave. I couldn't stand it.

Her gaze drifted past my shoulder, then landed back on me. *Right, she asked you a question.* I cleared my throat. "I think you went through a lot and that's bound to mess with your head."

"You didn't answer my question."

"I know."

Billie grimaced, running her fingers over the pendant I gave her for her birthday. The birthday we never celebrated because that asshole Daria and her friends snatched her up and locked her away. One of these days, when she was feeling better, I planned on taking Billie out on a proper date to celebrate. Maybe doing the things we used to do will help clear everything up and get her back on track. Hopefully.

"How could I just be making her up?" Billie asked, jarring me from my thoughts. "It seems impossible. I mean, Peyton and Morgan were a thing. And Peyton really cared about her, loved her maybe. At least, she did as far as I remember."

I tucked a loose strand of hair behind her ear. "People don't forget the ones they love, babe. I could never forget you."

She looked like I slapped her in the face, and I cringed at the expression she shot my way. It was somewhere between anger and disgust, and it made me feel like I was failing her all over again. I couldn't think of one thing to say that was right, it seemed, though, in my defense, this was an unprecedented situation with zero instruction on how one should act. Do I comfort her? Do I tell her the truth? Or do I play along with whatever delusions she might have? Each option was worse than the last, and I found myself playing with her hair and saying nothing at all instead.

"So, the only other explanation is that I made her up like I did Naomi, and I'm totally insane. That's just awesome."

"I know it might feel that way, and that it's scary, but this Morgan isn't someone we knew. Maybe you have her confused with someone else? Someone from Stamwick or something?"

She shook her head. "No. That definitely isn't it. Morgan was a witch hunter, like you. She was your friend for a long time, and a few months ago, she and Peyton got together. It happened right after Peyton got hurt while we were in Stamwick getting the Book of Darkness. Please, tell me that at least is real?"

"Well, that part is. That was when I gave you that." I pointed to the pendant on her neck and smiled. "And Peyton did get hurt."

"What about Savannah and Abigail? They were best friends with Morgan for years."

Nausea filled my mouth and I swallowed it down. "It was always just the two of them, at least as far as the hunting thing goes. I'm sorry, babe."

Billie frowned and I frowned with her. She was right about one thing. None of this made any sense. Not in the slightest.

"So, to sum up, everything else lines up except my memories of Morgan." She sighed. "I'm definitely going freaking crazy here."

"You're not," I assured her. "And I'm not discounting that you honestly believe this Morgan existed. But you're exhausted, babe, and you need some sleep. When was the last time you let yourself relax?"

She shrugged.

"See? You know, I've read that sleep deprivation can make you think and see things that aren't really there. As if your mind is trying to cope by making up a different world or something."

"Yeah, that sounds like someone going whacko to me," she scoffed.

"No," I argued. "More like someone needs to give themselves time to get over what they've been through."

Billie's eyebrows arched when she looked at me. "So, you're saying I have what? Cavern PTSD?"

I chuckled, surprised when she smiled in return. It was so nice to see her smile again.

"That's one way of putting it. Now, come on. Let's get you home and to bed."

"It's four in the afternoon..."

"You haven't slept in a week. And trust me, once school starts, you'll be grateful to have an afternoon of doing nothing but napping and eating. How about you go inside, and I'll go pick us up dinner from the Handsome Devil for later?"

After a long hesitation, Billie agreed, planting a soft kiss on my lips before climbing out of the car. Even her lips tasted sad, and my gut twisted at the thought of what she might be thinking. I couldn't imagine what I would do if the tables were reversed, and I couldn't help but feel proud of my girl for handling it so well. Sure, she was upset and confused, but still, I'd be tearing up the town if I was in her shoes. Billie was always so level-headed and strong that I couldn't imagine her not coping.

Maybe this time was different.

When I saw her duck into the house, I pulled out of the driveway and headed for Main Street, determined to brighten up her mood the only way I knew how. With a shit ton of food and constant reassurance that I was there for her no matter what. If Billie created make belief friends we didn't have, I had to step up my game and make sure she remembered the important bits.

I was going to remind her of everything good she had in this town until she realized that fake-Morgan was irrelevant. I would bring her back to reality if it was the last thing I did.

Chapter Three

Billie

Anyone that ever said they hated high school probably didn't get tortured by shifters and fae magic for a week. If they did, they'd know how to appreciate the loud clamor of students gossiping in the halls before the class bell rang out. Being someone that had a taste for the finer things, like not dying in a freaking cave, I knew exactly how wonderful being back in school was.

The shiny marble floors, the tan lockers, hell, even the assignments the teachers gave us to complete over the break made me giddy. After what I've been through, returning to Shadowhurst Academy was a blessing I wasn't going to take lightly.

My heart skipped a few beats as I rushed after Peyton with a lukewarm coffee cup in my hand. Unfortunately, River wasn't in any of my classes this semester, but Peyton and I still had first period together, and despite it being geometry, I couldn't wait to get started.

Skidding across the polished flooring, I rounded the corner to catch up with my best friend. Peyton's bright red streaks bounced behind her as she darted around a group of students, turning only slightly to make sure I was keeping up. We were late, as usual. As much as I hated not showing up on time, I had to admit that chasing after my friend without a care in the world was a refreshing change from the last week. In fact, I was pretty certain having my hair set on fire would have been a welcome change at this point. Anything but that damn cavern again.

A door swung open a foot away from me and I had to grind my heels to avoid smashing into it. My coffee cup jiggled in my hand, tossing a handful of milky brown all over my brand new white button-up.

Just flipping awesome.

I grimaced, inspecting the stain that was sure to ruin any hope I had of making a good first impression with Mrs. Sealie, our new teacher, and started after Peyton again.

Before I could bolt after her, my eyes landed on the tall, slim figure standing in the doorway beside me. "Oh, hey, Savannah," I said with a forced smile. "That was a close call."

"I see nothing changed since your first day here," the hunter scoffed. Savannah's shoulders dropped and she flashed her teeth my way. "Kidding, obvi. Why are you in such a hurry?"

I nudged my head in Peyton's direction, drawing Savannah's attention to my best friend's annoyed expression. Her sneaker tapped on the floor, and she was pointing to her watch, motioning for me to hurry. I shook my head and turned back to Savannah, letting out an exasperated sigh. "We're late. As always."

"I wouldn't stress about it," Savannah offered. "No one shows up on time in this place."

"Yeah, tell that to Peyton."

The hunter laughed and arched an eyebrow, looking me up and down. "Thought it was you that was always eager to get places?"

"HA!" I choked out. "Used to be, I guess. Things are... different now."

My gaze slid past Savannah to the empty classroom behind her. It was odd to see the hunter without her entourage, and I had to do a double-take around the room to make sure our friends weren't with her. Tentatively, I returned my focus to her and pursed my lips. "Where's everyone else?"

"Ugh," Savannah breathed out. "Abigail and Tyler are skipping today. Don't ask why because I can assure you, you do not want to know! Jayden is somewhere around, probably hitting on some poor junior girl and striking out as usual."

"What about—" I stopped myself before I could finish the question.

In front of me, Savannah tensed but pretended not to know what I was going to ask. *Thank the Goddess.*

"Anyway," I said after a long pause, "I better get over there before Peyton has a heart attack. See you at lunch?"

Savannah shook her head. "I want to hit up the house today. Logan needs all the help he can get with his pathetic fighting skills."

"You two getting close, huh?"

"Not what you're thinking," Savannah answered quickly. A little too quickly. "He's all right. When I don't want to kill him, that is. The rest of our stupid friends are still on vacay mode and he's the only one that wants to train, so here we are."

I decided not to press her further, and not because

Peyton was screeching for me to move it down the hallway. River had filled me in on the weirdness between Savannah and Logan and how close they seem to have gotten in the last week. If something was going on with those two, Savannah would share when she was ready. Until then, it was none of my business. I knew better than to press Savannah Michaels for information she wasn't ready to give. She and I were finally in a good spot, and I wasn't about to ruin it with my pathetic need for gossip. Besides, if there was anything worth knowing, Peyton would fill me in. My best friend was a walking tabloid magazine when it came down to Shadowhurst dirt.

Waving good bye to Savannah, I hurried over to a very cross Peyton and followed her to class. We cleared the stairs two steps at a time and ran into the classroom with only minutes before the bell rang. To our relief, the teacher was running behind and Peyton wiped the sweat off her brow before turning to me.

"You have got to be kidding me!" she yelled. "All that and this chick is late? Does she know I hate running? Because someone needs to make that clear. So unprofesh."

She tugged at my sleeve, dragging me behind her to the last row of seats in the back. Eyes watched us as we passed, and every student studied me with increasing interest. I couldn't really blame them. Between Peyton's outburst and my coffee-stained shirt, we sure knew how to make an entrance. Cheeks flushed, I scooted into the seat and placed a notebook on the table. My gaze fluttered over the classroom, a jolt of happiness spreading in my chest.

This was the same classroom I sat in on my first day at Shadowhurst Academy.

Memories of that day flashed before me, and I smiled

each time River's face appeared in my thoughts. Even on that first day, before knowing anything about me, he was kind. That was the thing about River. He always made me feel safe. Unlike Savannah, who couldn't have been a bigger bitch that day. Just thinking about it made resentment boil in my gut and I had to shake the feeling off, reminding myself that we were friends now and everything was fine. Still, I couldn't forget the way she treated me when I first came here. Or the way she and the other girls snickered when I walked by.

As soon as I pictured the girls, my heart dropped. My attention snapped to the desks closest to the front, narrowing on one in particular. The desk Morgan occupied when I sat in this exact classroom all those months ago. The one she used to draw on as the teacher droned on and on about some lesson no one cared for.

Pushing up, I ran past Peyton and toward Morgan's old desk. My heart raced in my chest, beating so wildly, I worried it might stop altogether. Pumping my legs, I reached the desk in seconds, ignoring the confused look of the student currently occupying it.

"Can I help you?" the boy asked, but I barely heard him.

All my attention was on the tabletop. Dragging a shaking hand over the wooden surface, I nudged his notebooks aside, ignoring his annoying protests. Not far from us, Peyton called my name, but I was too entranced to answer. My throat tightened and tears pricked at the back of my lids as I ran my gaze over the desk. The spotless, free of any markings desk.

How is that possible?

My mind raced as I checked the wood again, eyes darting over its surface. I couldn't have been making this up. The memory was so clear, I knew it had to be real. Yet there was nothing here. Why? Why was there no trace of Morgan's drawings? She drew on this desk so much, I was positive it'd be covered in her doodles.

Unless someone cleaned it?

Head spinning, I inspected the other desks in the classroom. Each one was filled with sketches and carvings students left behind in an attempt to make their presence here remembered. They had cleaned none of those desks, so why this one? Why the one I remembered Morgan sitting at?

I blinked, tearing my eyes off the desk and smiling sheepishly at the boy sitting in it. His eyes were bewildered like he was trying to see if I was all right while also wondering what the hell kind of headcase I truly was. With him still watching me, I made my way back to my seat and slouched down. Something was going on in this school and for some reason, I couldn't leave it alone. Sure, I was traumatized as heck from the cavern, but this was different. I just couldn't shake the fact that Morgan was real.

"You okay, B?" Peyton asked.

I cast a sideways glance her way, lowering my eyes back to my lap. "I don't think so. Something is seriously wrong with me."

Chapter Four

Billie

*L*aughter filled the quad in front of the academy as students trickled out for lunch break. Some gathered in large groups while others kept to themselves, carrying loads of books and keeping their heads down. Likely the junior students who were still getting used to the dynamic of the school and not knowing how to fit into it. *Good luck, kids. This place is a zoo.*

I smiled, leaning my head on River's shoulder and taking a giant bite out of the sandwich Thomas prepared that morning. Out of all the things I missed while I was in that stupid cavern, his cooking was in my top five. The man was a genius in the kitchen, and Imala was a lucky woman to have him. I guess I was lucky now too since I got to partake in every magical creation the wannabe chef concocted on the daily.

My stomach grumbled as I chewed, and River chuckled under my weight. "You are an insatiable pit," he said with a laugh.

"Spoken like someone who has no clue what he's missing," I threw back, waving the sandwich in his face. "Jealous?"

I was about to take another bite when a set of teeth curled around my precious cargo and ripped a piece off.

"What the hell, Jayden?" I shouted. "That is not for sharing!"

"Don't be waving things around you don't want to be eaten," Jayden retorted, chewing loudly. "And she's right, bruh. You should totally be jealous!"

"I wouldn't keep eating that if I were you," Peyton teased. "Never know where this boy's mouth has been."

She punched Jayden's shoulder and pushed her plastic container of noodles in my direction. Without hesitation, I tossed my abused lunch in Jayden's lap and rolled my eyes. *So freaking rude.*

Ten minutes later and Peyton and I devoured the last of her meal, leaning on the grass with satisfied grins on our faces. The sun beat down on our heads and the chatter of students continued to blast around us as we relaxed for the rest of lunchtime. Everything about this moment brought me so much joy, I could barely contain it. It was great to be back with my friends, greater still to be a regular student with no other worries in the world. As much as I loved being a witch, having moments like this where I was nothing more than a normal student in a human high school reminded me of what life was really about. It wasn't about magic and fighting supernatural evils. What life was, what it truly represented, was friendship and a sense of family. Something I didn't have before I met the oddballs that sat next to me now. It was freaking glorious.

"So, what was up with you in class this morning?" Peyton asked.

And just like that, my bubble shattered. *Just damn brilliant.*

I scrunched my forehead and stared past her at a group of students tossing a football around. "Nothing. I got confused."

"What happened?" River eyed the two suspiciously.

Thanks, girl. Now you got him going. "It wasn't a big deal, babe. I thought I remembered something, but I was wrong."

"Is this about..." Jayden said, pausing briefly. "That girl you think we knew?"

I nodded.

"What did you think you remembered?"

Sighing, I recounted the morning's events to my friends, avoiding the heated glare River trained on me the entire time I was speaking, or the looks Peyton threw my way. By the time I finished, my friends had gaping jaws and expressions that told me they had no idea what to say. I couldn't blame them. If someone told me they remembered a person I didn't think existed, I'd be as worried as them.

"Girl, trust me," Jayden finally said, breaking the awkward silence. "If there was a sultry redhead in this school, I'd know her. I love me some fiery females."

"Gross," Peyton murmured under her breath. "And you love pretty much every female you meet. Too bad none of them love you back."

Jayden pressed a palm to his heart, pretending to be hurt by her comment. "Ouch. Shots fired."

My friends laughed while my vision grew glassy.

A pair of muscular arms wrapped around my middle and pulled me into a tight embrace. "Hey, come on," River whispered against my ear. His breath tickled my neck and I shivered at the touch, remembering how much I missed this when I was apart from him. "Whatever effect that fae magic is having on you, we'll figure it out. Just try not to think about it for now."

Easy for you to say. You're not the one with Morgan's ghost haunting you.

"Why are you so sure it's fae magic?" I asked.

"What else could it be?"

I twisted to look at him. "I don't know, but it could be anything. Could be that I'm right."

River's features darkened and I noticed our friends sit up taller to listen. They still thought I was making it all up and it drove me nuts. Hell, maybe I was crazy, and Morgan never existed. In my pocket, the staurolite that reminded me of Naomi grew heavy and I shifted uncomfortably in River's hold.

"Maybe you guys are right," I said, grimacing. "I probably need to let it go."

"At least until Vic figures out what's causing this," Peyton offered.

"Yeah, you're right. It has to be some weird fae crap. That's the only thing that makes sense."

A football flew past me and landed at Jayden's feet, making all of us jump. In a flash, a short brunette was leaning over our group, her eyes apologetic as she reached to pick up the ball. Her focus drifted past the three of us and landed straight on Jayden, whose Cheshire smile made Peyton groan in disgust.

"I'm so sorry!" the girl exclaimed. "Didn't mean to hit you."

She leaned further, revealing way too much of her cleavage to my friend. He didn't seem to mind. Obviously.

"No worries, milady," Jayden said with a wink. "Mind if I join you guys?"

The girl beamed, flashing her teeth before leading him away from our group to join her friends. As they departed, Jayden turned, wiggling his eyebrows like the fool he was, and a loud laugh escaped me. He was about to turn around when Peyton chucked his varsity jacket at his chest.

"Don't forget the panty dropper!" she yelled out.

I cringed and River half-smiled. "Give the guy a break," he said to Peyton. "He's just lonely."

"Everyone's lonely," my best friend scoffed. "This is high school."

Her words made me think of Morgan and the relationship Peyton lost that she didn't even realize she had. When I first met Peyton, she was spunky and full of attitude, but her demeanor changed after she and Morgan got together. At least as far as I remembered. While it was nice to have my carefree, hot-blooded friend back, I wished that Morgan was real so Peyton could be happy with someone again. It was as though Peyton had changed somehow. I couldn't quite put my finger on it, but she wasn't the same girl I knew only days ago. She was different, only in the smallest of ways, but different nonetheless. I really wished I could tell her how strong she was with Morgan at her side.

But that wasn't happening.

Morgan didn't exist. I made her up the same way I made up Naomi. It was as though I had developed a creepy-ass defense mechanism for when shit hit the fan, and this time, I wasn't about to let my mind get away from me. This was nothing like the cavern. I was back in Shadowhurst with everyone I cared about, and I had to keep focusing on that fact.

No more pretend friends and no more crazy thoughts. I needed to concentrate on reality, and no matter how badly I wanted to believe Morgan was real, she simply wasn't.

This was my reality. Peyton's quirky personality, River's arms around my waist, and a busy quad full to the brim with carefree students.

Whatever my unstable mind wanted me to believe didn't matter. If not for any other reason than because I couldn't let it drag me off course. I wasn't sure why I was stirring up trouble where there wasn't any, but it was stopping today. I had finally gotten everything I wanted and no amount of crazy would take it away.

Leaning my shoulders against River's chest, I closed my eyes, letting the sun caress my skin in its warmth.

I was home. Finally. And I was going to make damn sure I stayed here, no matter what threatened to pull me away. *Not today, Satan. Not to-freaking-day.*

Chapter Five

River

To say that I was freaking the hell out was the understatement of the century. The pressure on my temples drummed a furious beat and made my jaw clench so tight, I had to ball my fists to keep from screaming. I really thought being back at school would make Billie come to her senses, but it seemed to have done the exact opposite.

My girl was spiraling and despite her acting like she agreed with us about the whole Morgan situation, I knew she was lying.

Billie hadn't been herself since we broke her out of that damn cave, and I was starting to think this wouldn't be as quick a fix as we first assumed it was. Whatever was messing with her head wasn't going away anytime soon and being in school only made things worse. After lunch, I pulled Peyton aside to tell me exactly how Billie acted that morning, and from the sounds of it, she was basically behaving like a lunatic.

My chest tightened as I leaned on the hood of my car and waited for the girls to get out of class so I could take

27

Billie home. We all thought she needed rest, but maybe that was the wrong approach. Leaving her alone was not doing her any favors. All it did was make her retreat further into herself and I hated to think that one day, she would stop sharing her thoughts with me altogether. What bothered me even more was that ever since she came back from the cave, the black lines I thought signaled our mate bond had not returned. Everything was falling apart, and I couldn't think of one thing to do to make it better.

There was no fixing Billie. Not when she didn't seem to want my help.

Around me, the parking lot grew less hectic as students left for the day, each one more eager than the first to get to wherever they were heading. My jealousy crept to the surface as I listened to their stories of the break, and my headache intensified from the continuous babbling. If only these morons knew what was out there, hiding in the dark and waiting to kill them. Except they didn't. They knew nothing at all, and their nonchalant behavior made me want to rip their throats out. *Lucky assholes.*

My fingers curled around the metal of the car, and I gritted my teeth to keep my feelings in check. Inside, the wolf whined, hating being cooped up for so long. I hadn't shifted in days and the effects were catching up with me. Every minute I spent pushing the wolf down felt like a ticking bomb, and I worried that if I didn't shift soon, someone around me would come to regret it. But shifting wasn't going to happen. At least not until I knew Billie was okay and I could leave her alone long enough to give myself a breather.

To make matters worse, I hadn't spoken to the pack since they refused to choose me as their alpha and the wolf definitely did not like that. Not that I cared. He would have to deal with the fact that it was just me and him from now on. Of course, he wasn't dealing with it as wonderfully as I had hoped. His incessant whining keeping me up until the late hours each night. Life was just freaking perfect.

I swear this town is going to eat me alive one of these days.

A loud laugh pierced the hilltop, and I narrowed my eyes on Peyton's slight figure in the distance. She was carrying on about something while Billie and Savannah trailed behind her with blank expressions on their faces. My gaze immediately snapped to my girl, and I struggled to reach her with my mind to see what she may have been thinking. As always, I drew a blank. Billie was unreachable, even from this short distance, and it made the disappointment of our lost bond that much greater. It was as if she was blocking herself from me and the rest of the world. *Fucking perfect.*

"Squeeze any tighter and you'll dent the metal," a soft voice sounded behind me.

I turned, finding Victoria's sharp eyes trained on my tense hands. The witch appeared out of nowhere, as she often did, and I cringed at the sight of her. One thing I learned so far was that wherever Victoria was, trouble was sure to follow. This girl was the bearer of bad news, and if she was paying us an unannounced visit at school, there had to be a reason for it. A reason I was not eager to hear.

"Hey," I said. "What are you doing here?"

Victoria frowned. "Something's come up."

Of course, it freaking did. "What?"

"Let's wait for everyone else. I want Billie to hear this."

I arched an eyebrow but didn't push her further. Instead, I uncurled my fingers from the hood and turned my attention back to Billie as she made her way down the hill toward us. As soon as she saw Victoria, her face lit up and she sped up. Even from here, I could see the nerves building up behind her eyes and worry set into the creases of her brow. Billie had asked Victoria to look into what was wrong with her, and I couldn't blame her for being eager to get some answers. Though, I knew better. Whatever the witch came here to tell us, it would not be anything good. Victoria's face told me that much.

"You got nothing on what's going on with her, do you?" I asked, my eyes never leaving Billie.

Next to me, Victoria lowered her gaze to the floor.

"Perfect."

We waited in silence until the girls made their way down the lot, surrounding us with expectant glares. Peyton's head swerved between Victoria and I like she was trying to read our minds while Savannah crossed her arms over her chest and scanned the cars to make sure no one overheard us. But it was Billie I couldn't stop watching. Her chest rose and fell as she inspected Victoria, and every second that passed when no one spoke seemed to drain her of energy. Unable to keep seeing her suffer, I peeled myself off the car and closed the distance between us. My hands reached for hers, holding them tightly as I searched her eyes. Billie's gaze darkened, asking the silent question we all had on our minds.

I shook my head, letting her disappointment stab into my heart. "Nothing yet. I'm sorry, babe."

"It's okay," she said. "I'm okay."

You so aren't.

Billie wiggled her hands away from mine and shoved them in her leather jacket. I immediately regretted not holding on tighter. Her head swiveled to peer past me at

Victoria and she half-smiled. The emptiness of her false happiness dragged me down and I tried to keep my expression as blank as possible, with little success. *How can I help you, love? How can I make this better?*

"Good to see you, Vic," Billie said, pulling me away from my own thoughts. "You really have nothing on this?"

"Not yet," Victoria answered. "But I'll keep looking. We'll figure it out. There's something else, though."

"Ugh. What now?" Savannah asked, rolling her eyes dramatically.

Victoria shifted her weight from foot to foot like she was considering bolting. At her awkwardness, my body tensed, and I tried not to let my agitation reach Billie.

"It's the coven. I have some friends left there I can trust, witches that have loyalty to my family," Victoria said. "The high priestesses are up to something."

"What in the name of sweet hell are those bitches up to now?" Peyton shrieked.

All four of us shushed her in unison, and Peyton's cheeks flared as she realized her mistake. There were still a few students left in the lot, and while her outburst didn't draw much attention, we couldn't take any risks. Looking around, Peyton lowered her voice to a whisper. "Seriously, though, don't tell me no one else is over them?"

To my surprise, Billie laughed and nudged her friend's side. "Second that," she said, still chuckling. "So what have Sebyl and her group of monsters been up to?"

"My friend didn't know. But she said they've been keeping away from everyone. Same with the head witches. And they moved up seven initiations this month. Her little sister was supposed to get initiated next year, and her mom showed up last night to tell them it was happening in two weeks instead. Every witch that was scheduled to be in as a junior is to be initiated on the next full moon. It's freaky. I don't trust them."

"Why would they bring in more junior witches right now?" Billie asked. "They're just kids."

Savannah sighed. "Building a bigger army, maybe?"

"Maybe..." Billie said. "But with young witches? That doesn't make any sense. Those girls don't have enough magic to wield the elements. They'd literally be the worst army ever. This doesn't sound good."

"My thoughts exactly," Victoria said, nodding. "I'm going to keep checking, see if I can dig up something else. And I promise I haven't forgotten about your little problem."

The way she said 'problem' made the hairs on my arms rise and I could sense Billie's discomfort matching my own. Her mind going bonkers wasn't a problem, it was a freaking disaster, and we all knew it.

"Thanks, Vic," Billie said, her fake smile hanging limp on her lips. "Text me as soon as you have something. In the meantime, someone should tell the resistance to keep their eyes open. We don't know what the coven might do next."

"On it," Peyton said and twirled the ring of her car keys over her index finger. "I'll go there now. My dad's working late today, so this prisoner has a few hours to spare before he checks in."

"I'll follow you there," Savannah offered.

The two got into their cars and peeled out, leaving us in a cloud of dust and smoke in the parking lot. When they were gone, Victoria turned back to Billie and me, her face unreadable as it often was. The witch twirled her ponytail in her fingers, pulling it out as far as it could reach before letting it drop. "Remember that spell we did back in the day to mess with Courtney?"

Billie's eyebrows rose and my shoulders sagged. "Who's Courtney?"

"Another junior witch in the coven," Billie answered.

"Total bitch," Victoria added. "Anyway, Billie and I had enough of her crap, so we found a spell to screw with her mind a little. Nothing dangerous, but it made her think she saw things that weren't there."

"What kind of things?"

"Nothing major. Just like shadowers where there weren't any and some other fun stuff."

Victoria's definition of 'fun stuff' was very different from my own. Very. Damn. Different.

"Vic," Billie said, forehead scrunching. "I know what you're thinking, and it won't work. That was a mirage spell. And it only lasted a couple of hours."

"I know, I know. But what if you change it up a bit? Target the memory of this chick you're stuck on and instead of amplifying it, erase it? It's worth a shot. At least until I figure out something else."

Next to me, Billie's back uncurled and she squared her shoulders. "I guess. But if this is the result of fae magic I know nothing about, it probably won't work."

"What if it does work? You have to try it, babe."

"Okay, yeah. I'll give it a shot. If anything, maybe I could erase those memories for a few hours and get some sleep for a change. This is good."

Nothing about this was good, but it was the first glimpse of hope I felt in days, so I was willing to go with it. Maybe this spell would actually work, and Billie would be herself again. Then again, the whole thing could backfire, and she could end up in even worse shape than she was before. Just in case, I decided to stay close to her place for the remainder of the evening, which wasn't as creepy as it sounded. Okay, fine, it was creepy as shit, but I didn't care. If this spell didn't work, Billie would need me there and it would be a snowy day in Hell before I let her out of my sight again. The news on the High Coven Victoria delivered made me uneasy. Something was brewing and I couldn't let my guard down right now. None of us could.

Things were about to get interesting. *What a shit show.*

Chapter Six

Billie

he potent smell of wormwood and angelica filled my bedroom as I ground the herbs into a fine powder in the small bowl in my lap. My nostrils tickled from the sharp aroma and my eyes wetted as the fumes burrowed into my throat. There was no way to know if Vic was onto something with this spell, but I had to at least try. What did I have to lose at this point? My sanity was already down the drain.

I reached for the small knife on the floor beside me and pricked my index finger with its tip. Letting the blood drip into the bowl, I closed my eyes and willed my mind to clear. The surrounding air thickened and I could feel it wrap over my skin as my blood blended with the powdered herbs. When I couldn't stand it anymore, I shoved my finger in the bowl and mixed the contents into a thick paste before tracing the rune I needed to complete the spell on the wooden floorboards beneath me.

Tentatively, I eyed my creation and frowned. My art skills could sure use a refresher because this rune looked like a hot mess. It was close enough, so I knew it would likely work, but still, what an embarrassment. If Luna was here, she'd have scolded me for this pathetic attempt at drawing. Granted, if she was here, I'd have a different problem on my hands.

I shook the thoughts away, clearing my head once more, and pressed my palm over the rune. Deep down, my magic tingled and the hairs on my neck rose as it rushed to the surface. Goddess, how I missed this feeling.

Little by little, I gathered the magic into a tight ball, envisioning it rise from my gut and into my fingertips. Its energy pulsed against my skin as magic pushed through me, surrounding the crooked rune under my palm.

My body shook and my head pounded while I fought to keep the magic's direction in place. Closing my eyes, I searched for the spell's elements, clutching to it like the greedy bastard I was. When I could feel the elements under my fingers, I let the magic loose and waited for the spell to blast me with its power. If this worked, I should feel the pressure on my head lessen and my thoughts should grow foggy from its effects. *Any second now. Any... damn... second.*

Peeling one eye open, I looked down and frowned.

Nothing.

Frustrated, I tried again, this time loosening my control on the magic. Maybe I was overthinking this. Maybe all I had to do was let go and the elements would do the rest. Maybe—

A blast of power hit my chest and I fell back, toppling to the floor. My eyes snapped open, and I watched in horror as shadows tore from my fingers and wrapped around the small rune next to my feet. My mind raced and I reached for them, trying to pull them back into myself. Instead, the shadows rose higher, swirling over me in a tornado of energy and anger. My hair whipped over my face as a gust of wind raised me off the ground and carried me upward. My legs kicked out under me, and I worked to bring myself back down without success.

In my chest, my heart pounded like a drum, and panic set in.

Before I could do anything else, something wet dripped down my forehead and I yanked my gaze up to look to the ceiling. Jaw slacking, my eyes widened as a massive cloud formed over my head. It grew darker and darker, taking away any other light in my bedroom with its storm. All around me, the wind picked up, blowing out the few candles I had lit to perform the spell. Thunder cracked over me and I shielded my head as heavy rain broke from the cloud. The entire room rumbled, and terror set in when I realized the earth was shaking beneath the guest house.

My breath quickened and my pulse raced in my veins while I watched magic wreak havoc on my room. The shadows spread over my legs and arms, pulling my body upward in mid-air like a marionette. Above me, the thunder cracked again, and I shut my eyes, praying for the Goddess to save me.

What the hell was happening?

"Stop!" I screamed. "STOP NOW!"

My lids fluttered and I balled my fists, reaching for the shadows as best I could. Instantaneously, I struggled to connect to the other elements around me, and when I felt their ridges at the back of my mind, I pictured wrapping my fingers around them. One by one, I reeled the elements in, pulling them out of the room and back into my body. The puffy cloud above me brightened and dissipated, the wind died down, and the room stopped trembling. When the last of the shadows crawled back inside, I plummeted to the floor with a yelp. My knees hit the wood and an agonizing pain ran up my thighs.

I slumped to the side, hugging my knees into my chest, and dared to open my eyes again.

The room was a damn mess.

There were dents in the walls and everything I owned was soaking wet. My books were strewn all over the floor and a few picture frames had shattered across the carpet.

"What the..."

Darting my eyes over the destruction, I forced myself to sit up and ran shaking fingers through my knotted hair. What just happened here? I was in control and then the magic just exploded. It was like every element around me wanted to come out and play, but that wasn't possible. I didn't reach for them, and I didn't ask for their power. This was something beyond me, something I had no command of. Something that scared me shitless.

A loud knock sounded at the front door, and I bolted for it. Turning the knob, I quickly straightened my clothes and brushed my hair back, though I knew I still looked like a drowned rat despite my efforts. The door creaked open, and a worried Silas stood on my doorstep. His eyes narrowed on my destroyed appearance as he titled his gold-rimmed glasses on the bridge of his nose to get a better look.

"Is everything all right here, Billie?" he asked, his gaze looking me up and down. "Was there an accident?"

"No!" I yelped. Then daring to look down at the pool of water dripping from my sneakers, "I mean, yes. Nothing to worry about, though. I had a little run-in with the shower head when I tried to turn it on."

"Oh, I will take care of that for you. This place has a mind of its own sometimes."

Silas pushed his way past me, and I had to all but body-check him out of the way. "It's really nothing, Silas. I swear. I'm an idiot and everything is fine now. Plus, my room is a mess. Trust me, you do not want to see what a pig I am."

Silas smiled but didn't back away.

"I promise," I urged. "If it happens again, I'll let you know."

Reluctantly, Silas took a step back before peering over my shoulder. "Mr. and Mrs. Chandler will be home in an hour, I will call for you when dinner is ready."

"Thanks, Silas!" I yelled out at his departing back and closed the door.

My shoulders sagged and I leaned against the doorway, letting my body slump down to the ground. Still shaking, I reached into my jean pocket and pulled out the small stone I hid there, flipping it between my fingers like I was performing a magic trick at a kid's birthday party.

"I think I'm broken, Naomi," I whispered to the stone. "I seriously think I'm broken."

Tears pooled behind my eyelids and no matter how hard I tried, I couldn't push them away. They poured down my cheeks as I slumped to my knees and let my fear and confusion flow out of me. Not only was I losing my mind, but I was also losing my grasp on magic, and it scared me so deeply, I didn't know what to do with myself. What happened to me in that cavern? More importantly, how was I going to fix it? I was a danger to myself and with my magic going haywire, I was a danger to everyone else too. It was as though Billie was gone and something else took her place, and whatever that thing was, I was certain it would be the end of me.

39

Crawling on all fours, I dragged myself to the couch, leaving a trail of water in my wake. For all my life, magic defined me. It made me strong, and it made me fearless. Yet now, I have feared nothing more. Whatever it was I was turning into, it was going to destroy every inch of me unless I figured out how to stop it.

The worst part was I didn't know how to make it go away. I didn't even know where to start.

Chapter Seven

Billie

*W*hen the phone rang that evening, I all but fell off my bed from the sound. After eating dinner with the Chandlers, I sneaked away and spent the rest of the night cleaning up the mess left behind in my bedroom. Every broken glass and torn book I threw away sent shivers down my spine. I couldn't believe my magic did all this. That was exactly why, when River called to invite me out for a late-night get together with our friends, I had to say yes.

I needed to get out of this place before my head exploded.

Sunset spread over the backyard and cast an ominous orange glow over my room, tinting it a shade so close to spilled blood, it made my heart drop to my feet. Outside, leaves rusted on the multi-colored trees, and I ended up staring out the window like a freaking psycho for ten minutes straight. Shaking myself into alertness, I straightened my sweatshirt, frowning at the sad state of my attire. I knew River didn't care what I looked like, but if I had any chance of convincing our friends I wasn't certifiably nuts, I had to at least look presentable.

As I turned to head to the closet, a flash of movement in the backyard caught my eye and I froze in my spot.

My attention snapped to the edge of the pool, and I stood rigid as a board, narrowing my eyes to see clearer. The yard was as empty as ever, making me feel like an idiot immediately. My nerves had been sky high for days, and every shadow in the distance reminded me of the mysterious man that visited me in the cavern. The one that claimed to be my father. I still hadn't decided if he was a figment of my imagination or not, though judging by how things have been going, I was coming around to the notion that nothing in that stupid place was real, shadow man including.

Another quick glance around the yard and my nerves settled. There was no one there.

In my rear pocket, my cellphone vibrated, and my heart sped up when I read over River's last message.

Be there in ten.

SHIT!

Flying to the closet, I pulled down a stack of leggings, tossing them aside with a grunt. Every piece of clothing I owned was utilitarian, something I was quite proud of most of the time. A girl never knew when she needed to be ready to kick some ass, and leggings and tees were a great uniform for my lifestyle. Tonight, however, I wished I took Imala up on her continuous hints to take me shopping since one look at my closet told me I literally had nothing appropriate to wear. Sure, it wasn't as if we were going to some freaking ball, but still. River said Savannah arranged the get-together and knowing her, we would end up somewhere I felt completely out of place. *Spectacular.*

I rummaged through the shelves, pulling out shirt after shirt and groaning in disappointment. Honestly, would it have killed me to buy something colorful? Yep. It probably would have. For sure.

Maybe I can glamor an outfit?

Flashes of my magic exploding just hours ago rushed over me and I stifled the thoughts deep down where they couldn't bother me later. Magic was a hard 'no' right now.

The phone vibrated in my palms with another message from River, and my pulse sped up to a thundering beat. *In the front.*

DOUBLE DAMN IT!

Tapping on the keys, I typed out a message and returned my attention to the closet, desperation coating every part of me. Keeping River waiting was the last thing I wanted to do, and I was taking forever to get ready. If I didn't show up in the next five minutes, he'd be barging in here, thinking something was wrong. Refusing to let him worry any further, I tied my hair into a low ponytail and returned to my search.

My fingers wrapped over a pair of white pants that looked to be somewhat clean, and I smiled, tossing them on the bed as an option. One by one, I tore shirts off their hangers, trying to find something to match. Suddenly, in the closet's corner, a flash of color appeared, and I nearly jumped for joy when I saw it. My knees hit the floor and I crawled past the mountain of clothes I erupted to get to the one thing I knew would work for the occasion. Pulling at the silky fabric, I straightened the item, holding it up to the light.

When did I get this thing?

I eyed the tank top suspiciously, running my gaze over the yellows and pinks of the soft fabric. It was a simple scooped neck tank with a frilly bottom and thin spaghetti straps holding up a tiny sliver of fabric someone considered being good enough to call a shirt. This thing wouldn't cover enough of my skin by a long shot, and I wondered why the hell I bothered keeping it around. I couldn't remember wearing anything like this and was about to toss it to the side and opt for my standard band tee when a memory attacked my senses.

I was in my room. The sun glowed through the large windows and loud cackles sounded all around me. I turned my head, eyes widening as I watched the memory come to life before me. On the floor, Peyton sat cross-legged, holding up a small mirror to her face as she retraced the thick dark liner around her eyes with layers upon layers of kohl. Beside her, Abigail tried to braid Savannah's thick hair, cursing intermittently under her breath.

"Hold still, girl," she hissed, tugging Savannah's head backward. "If you keep moving, this is going to look like a disaster."

"It already looks like a disaster," Savannah bit back. "Learn when to stop."

"No go," Abigail sniped. "Girls' day means you have to play along."

"Just use your bow and arrow on her," Peyton teased, her concentration never leaving the work of art she was creating on her face. My best friend glanced at me briefly and winked before turning back to the mirror.

Tears stung the rear of my eyes as I remembered this day. Savannah and I were still on shit terms, but she was coming around, and having the other girls here helped. It was rare for all of us to spend much time together, and despite Savannah being here, I loved every second. Being with them made me feel like Shadowhurst wasn't the Hellhole I originally thought it was and that I could actually fit in here one day. Moments like these were rare, and even now, I still looked back on those days fondly.

"What is taking that girl so long?" Savannah asked, eyeing my closet. "You'd think we're going to a freaking gala with how long she's taking to get ready."

Just as she spoke, my closet doors burst open, and a spunky redhead walked through. My head spun and my mouth dried up as I watched Morgan appear in the room wearing one of my ripped band tees. Her eyes glittered mischievously and she balled up the flowery tank top she arrived in with her hands.

"I'm borrowing this," Morgan announced, leaving me no room to argue. "It's pretty sweet."

She looked at me, or through me maybe. I wasn't sure. All I saw was the silky ball of a shirt in her hands. All I saw were yellows and pinks and the smallest hint of ruffle at the bottom.

Morgan tossed the shirt in my closet and walked to sit next to the other girls. Her smile stretched from ear to ear when she settled next to Peyton, and the two of them said something out of earshot. Next to them, Savannah rolled her eyes and let Abigail continue attacking her curls.

The surrounding air thickened and my vision blurred. I reached for the wall, steadying myself, and swallowing the bouts of nausea that pushed up my throat. As the memory dissipated, leaving me alone in my room again, my eyes returned to the shirt in my hands. With sweaty fingers, I flattened out the fabric, eyes wide as saucers while I looked it over.

This was Morgan's tank top. She was here and she left it behind.

Hairs rose on the back of my neck and saliva pooled under my tongue. I wasn't crazy. Morgan was very real, and she was gone. Someone took her and I had to find her before something horrible happened. Somehow, I didn't know how, I sensed this was only the beginning. Whatever happened to Morgan wasn't the end of it, and I was the only one who could figure out what was going on. I was the only one who could bring her back.

Chapter Eight

Billie

"Y ou sure you don't want to hang out with everyone else tonight?" River asked, speeding down the winding streets of our sleepy town.

His eyes kept drifting to me each time we stopped at a light, and I tried to smile despite the urge to vomit that built up inside me. I hadn't told River about the tank top I found. In foresight, I likely should have, but I couldn't bring myself to do it. Everyone thought I was going insane, River including, and though I knew the top belonged to Morgan, even I had to admit it wasn't much in the way of proof. For all they knew, I bought the dumb shirt myself and just forgot about it.

That wasn't the case, of course. Still, it would only make me look crazier if I attempted to explain and as much as I hated lying to River, this was one time it needed to be done.

Which was why instead of filling him in on what I remembered, I told him I wanted to do some research on the fae to help Vic move things along. He didn't sway me otherwise, because he was the best, and offered to come with me to the Shadowhurst Archive Library. I believe 'the more eyes the better' was his actual sentiment on the matter. I wasn't sure how his eyes could be of use considering he had no clue I was actually searching for a person who didn't seem to exist anymore, but whatever. The library was closing soon, and if I biked there, I'd never make it in time. Having him drive us over was a huge blessing I wasn't going to argue with. Gift horse, mouth, and so on.

We rounded a corner and I slid in the car's passenger side, gripping the handle to keep steady. "I can't relax until I figure this out," I said. "Thanks for taking me."

"Where you go, I go," River said, and I melted into the leather seat.

There were only a handful of cars in the lot by the time we pulled in, which was fine by me. The fewer people around to see me unravel, the better.

Marching up the small steps to the front door, I could hear my pulse skyrocket under my skin as we made our way to the massive bookcases lining the library. There was so much history in these rooms, I had no idea where to look. To be honest, I wasn't even sure what I was looking for. Something that pointed to Morgan's existence in this town. Anything, really.

But where to start?

"So, where do you want to start?" River asked, taking the words out of my mouth.

"Um..." I looked around. "Why don't you see what you can find in the newspaper clippings, and I'll go this way?"

I didn't even know which direction I pointed, but it seemed to placate River and he followed my instructions without another word. When he was out of sight, I ran for a computer at the end of a long mahogany table and turned it on. My fingers danced over the keyboard as I struggled to think of something to type into the database.

"What now?" I asked myself, staring at the blank screen.

Not knowing how one goes about looking for a person erased from memory, I pulled up the first thing I could think of. Shadowhurst Academy yearbooks. The library had them neatly labeled by year, and I cringed when I saw how many there were. The yearbooks went back almost as far as fifty years ago, and I was certain there were physical books somewhere that dated even further. Luckily, I only needed the last few.

Hovering over one folder, I clicked to pull up the book from last year and scrolled through the photos. The academy housed almost eight hundred students, sometimes more, and there were a ton of people to sift through. I checked for Morgan's name first, coming up empty, then started going through each photo one by one. There was a chance she was documented under a different name. My logic was flawed at best, but I couldn't leave any stone unturned if I was going to find her.

After an excruciating twenty minutes, I still had nothing to go by.

None of the students matched Morgan's description, and I recognized most of the kids from our school. The yearbooks were a dead end. *Freaking fabulous.*

Clicking out of the search, I stared at the blinking cursor and groaned. "Where else?"

My mind raced as I attempted to come up with the next place to look when an idea hit me. I knew where Morgan lived. Granted, I've never been to her place, but I at least remembered the address. Thanks to the High Coven, the need to remember every bit of information I came across was pretty well ingrained in my personality. You never knew when you might need to pull up a spell on the go. Because of this, whenever I saw numbers or names, I was pretty damn good at committing them to memory. There wasn't much I was grateful to the coven for, but this was one trick up my sleeve I was glad to have at the moment.

Glancing around to make sure River was still preoccupied wherever he was, I searched for the town's real estate database. It hadn't been updated in a few years, but if memory served me right, River once said Morgan moved to Shadowhurst when they were younger. It made sense for her family's home to be listed here. Eagerly, I pounded the keyboard and entered the address into the search bar.

My heart leaped in my throat when a photo of her family's house popped on screen, and I clicked on the image to expand the details. According to the archives, the house went up for sale ten years ago; purchased by a couple from Stamwick who wanted to turn it into a Bed and Breakfast. There was no mention of Morgan's family ever owning the place, and to make matters worse, the couple that bought the house never followed through with the plan and it had been sitting empty for years. Apparently, the city was petitioning to buy it back from them, but the couple refused to sell, leaving the damn thing abandoned.

"For the love of!" I cursed, punching the keyboard with my fist.

"In the market for a house?" River asked and I jumped in my seat before turning to face him.

Attempting to wet my cracked lips, I gulped down spit and forced myself to calm down. "I... uh..." I struggled to come up with an excuse. "I fell down a rabbit hole, I think. Did you find anything?"

He shook his head 'no' and I noticed the frustration build behind his green eyes. I knew he wouldn't find anything. There was nothing to find. Still, seeing him this annoyed didn't make me feel great about lying to him. Unfortunately, there was a lot more lying I had to do in the next little while, so I had better get used to it.

"Well, thanks for coming with me, anyway. This was dumb, but I'm glad we did it. At least now I know there's nothing here," I said. *Technically, not a lie.* "We should probably go."

"I really wanted to find something," River said, his lips crashing into a thin line. "I want to help you. I really want to figure this out."

My heart broke for him, and I fought the urge to press my lips to his right that second. One look around told me this was not the best place for a make-out session. The last thing I needed was for the librarian to see me all over River and tell the Chandlers they let a hussy into their home. No, thank you. I intertwined my fingers with River's and gave his hand a light squeeze. "I know you do, and I want you to know I appreciate it. I'm glad I have you, you know? Not sure I could have handled this well if you weren't here."

River smiled and the tension in my neck eased up. "Besides," I added, "I actually feel much better now."

"Why don't I believe you?" he asked and arched a thick eyebrow my way.

"Honest! You guys were right, I was acting crazy before."

"No one said that."

I frowned. "Yeah, but everyone thought it. I did too. But I know what's real now, so you don't have to worry. Trust me, everything will be just fine." *Again, not a lie.*

"You sure?" River asked.

"One hundred percent!" I announced. "Think you can take me home? I'm pretty beat."

"Sure. Wanna watch a movie tonight?"

I started to agree when an idea formed in my head. "Actually, think I can take a rain check on that? Maybe tomorrow or something? I seriously might pass out in the first ten minutes."

River's laugh echoed through the hushed library, and he pulled me up, pressing a soft kiss to my lips before turning to lead me out. As I followed him to the car, I glanced back at the building and grinned. I was serious when I said I was tired. I was so damn tired of all of this that my brain was pure mush. Yet no matter how beat down I felt, there was something I had to do that would put my mind at ease and River couldn't come with me. He wouldn't understand.

I had to see Morgan's house for myself, abandoned or not. And I had to do it tonight.

Chapter
Nine

River

I left Billie at home and drove around mindlessly. Even though she said she was fine, I didn't believe her. Sure, she was acting more like herself again, but who knew what was going on in that brilliant brain of hers? After getting in my car, I had half the mind to turn around and barge into her room just to make sure she was resting as she should be, then thought better of it. Me acting a fool was not what Billie needed right now, and if she wanted a break for the night, I had to oblige.

Shifting the car to park, I looked up, realizing I drove to the entrance in the woods that led to the resistance without realizing it. Inside, the wolf growled in excitement, and I wanted to punch his stupid mouth. I had avoided this place like the plague since we got Billie back from fear of running into the pack, and I knew he wasn't happy about it. *Tough luck, moron. No furry friends for you.*

My phone buzzed on the dashboard, and I tapped the home button to wake it up.

A message from Raiden popped on the screen. *Is that you?*

Great. There went my plan to get the hell out of here before someone realized I stopped by. Typing a response, I got out of the car and inspected the dark line of trees lining the lot. There was a rustle near to me and in seconds, Raiden and Mel emerged from the trees.

"Thought that was your car," Raiden said. "Finally decided to come by, huh?"

I gritted my teeth. "Not really. I just dropped Billie off and ended up here."

"How is she doing?" Mel asked. The concern in her tone made my jaw tick.

"She's good. Much better now, I think. Whatever was going on seems to have gone away. At least I hope it did."

"That's great!" Raiden exclaimed and patted my shoulder.

"What are you guys even doing out here?" I asked. "It's late."

"We've been patrolling every night. All the leaders have, except Peyton. I don't think her dad is thrilled with her new position, so she's been having some trouble coming by. Maybe you can help us out instead."

"Yeah, no," I said sternly.

Raiden laughed. "How about a run in the forest then? For old time's sake."

"Also, no."

"Once a moody bastard, always a moody bastard."

My fists balled and I buried my feet into the ground to keep from attacking him. I knew Raiden was only teasing, but that didn't mean I had to like it. As always, it was up to Mel to ease the tension, and she looped around her mate to stand between us. Her black eyes reflected the moonlight as she peered up at me, a small smile tugging at her lips. "He's kidding. Don't let it get to you."

"I know," I said between clenched teeth. "And I'll shift again, just not yet."

"No pressure," Mel said in a hushed tone. "We get it. Don't we?"

She cast a dangerous glare at Raiden, and the larger-than-life shifter all but shrank in place. I had to hand it to Mel, she knew how to keep her guy wrapped around her finger. It was pretty amazing, actually.

Tearing my eyes from them, I scanned the trees. "So, who else is out here with you guys?"

"A couple of people from the house. Lorelei is around somewhere—"

Mel didn't get to finish her sentence when the mind reaper stepped out and strolled toward us. Her long legs carried her like a wave and her pale hair drifted down her back in the wind. Despite the dropping temperature, Lorelei was wearing her standard uniform. A long, silk dress that was so sheer, I wondered how she wasn't freezing her ass off in this weather. Somehow, none of it bothered Lorelei in the least. In fact, she looked to be more comfortable than any of us on this chilly night in the woods.

When she was halfway to us, another figure arose on the horizon, and I peered past her to see Logan stomp forward on her heels. The reaper's wide-set shoulders bounced as he closed the distance between himself and our group, flashing a row of pearly whites in my direction.

"Hey, mate. Came to join the fun?" Logan asked.

"Just driving by," I answered.

Beside him, Lorelei trained her violet eyes on me, and I

noticed for the first time they were almost the same shade as Logan's. Was every mind reaper this creepy looking or only these two? It was uncanny how much their stares resembled each other; as though they were looking right into your damn soul. I shook off their glares and looked down at my feet. "You guys do this every night?"

"We must keep our defenses ready," Lorelei responded. "It is impossible to tell what the High Coven will do next, and with people coming back to the house, it is best to be prepared."

"The shadowers are back in the house? All of them?"

"Some. Not all. Though we are hopeful more will return soon. We need to stay with our own kind, especially in times of danger."

Was that a hint? I tried not to think about it. I had no intention of being anywhere near my kind for as long as I could help it. Nope. Not by a long shot.

I was about to question her more when six shadowers stepped out to meet us. In the dark, it was hard to tell one face from the next, though I didn't need to see them to know who it was. The annoying excited yelps of the wolf inside me gave the pack away before I could even focus my eyes. It wasn't all of them, but there were enough to make my blood freeze and my legs tense. This was just my luck, to run into the very people I have been trying to avoid at the one place I swore I wouldn't come back to.

Stupid idiot!

Before me, Raiden and Mel watched my reaction with calculating eyes like they were trying to grasp my level of discomfort. It was a solid two hundred on a scale of one to ten. Still, there was no need for them to worry. I wasn't about to do anything stupid. This was simply inconvenient as hell.

It was like being forced to hang out with a girl you asked out after she rejected you. Super freaking awkward.

"Oh, goody," Logan teased, "more wolves. Yay!"

I shot him a side glance, but the moron didn't get the clue. *Perfect.*

"Hey, man," Griffin said when he was close enough for me to make out his face. "Long time."

"Yep." I nodded. "How've you been?"

I looked past his shoulder and searched for Isaac, but to my relief, he wasn't there. Recognizing some shifters, I offered a small smile to each of them, being welcomed with smiles in return. Despite how I imagined this going, the pack didn't seem to have a problem with me, which made me feel like a complete bastard. There was a very good chance I had to get over it and play nice already. So what if they rejected me and refused to accept me as their alpha? It wasn't like I went about it in the best way. I pretty much tried to shove myself down their throats, and if I was them, I wouldn't like that either. Thinking of my childish behavior didn't make me feel any less frustrated, so I focused on being as polite as possible instead.

It was a damn disaster.

"I see Isaac isn't here?" *Dude, ease up. Learn to be a person. Geez.* "I mean, is he still, you know..."

I was hopeless.

Griffin threw his head back and let out a loud laugh. "You need to chill, man. Isaac's still in the pack, but no, he's not the alpha anymore. We don't have one right now."

"Isn't that weird?" Logan asked.

Excellent question.

"Yep. Totally strange, but we're figuring it out. And no one's pissed at you," Griffin said. "If you decide to move on, you're more than welcome in the pack. Or at least help us with these damn patrols because I for one am hella tired of my nights being taken away. No offense, guys."

He glanced back to the shadower leaders, who all looked equally annoyed with his comment. Lorelei specifically. The mind reaper's eyes shot daggers at Griffin, and I wondered if he could feel her frustration pierce his skin. He definitely didn't and I couldn't help but laugh at the nonchalant attitude the kid had.

"Anyway," Griffin said, shrugging off the death glares around him. "We still run every morning at seven, if you ever want to join in."

My wolf whined and I mentally kicked him. *Shut. Up.* "Thanks," I said. "I'll think about it. And I can help with the patrols soon, just have something to take care of first."

"Yeah, we heard about Billie. If there's anything we can do to help, let us know."

"I will."

As I watched Griffin lead the pack into the dark woods, my body shivered. Desperately, I wanted to run after them and join the people that were, by default, supposed to be my closest friends. A part of me wanted to let myself escape with them, to join their shifts, and run free through the forest as the wolf I was meant to be. A bigger part of me wanted nothing to do with it. I didn't want to have people in my life tied to me by obligation alone. What I wanted was a sense of family. Something that got ripped away from me when my mom turned into a crazy-ass murderer. No matter what the wolf wanted, I wasn't supposed to have a pack. What I was supposed to have was Billie, and until she was fixed, I couldn't allow myself to think of my own desires.

I rubbed my chest, annoyed with the unblemished skin

under my shirt. Maybe until Billie gets better, I could work on finding out where those black lines went and why they haven't returned?

Perhaps I could fix her by fixing what broke with our bond. I knew Billie said not to jump to conclusions, but I couldn't get the lines out of my head. It had to be the mate bond. At that moment, I couldn't think of anything more pressing than figuring it out. I was going to make those damn lines come back and I was going to prove to her that we were meant to be together no matter what stood in our way.

Chapter Ten

Billie

*S*neaking down the nightly streets of Shadowhurst was probably the dumbest thing I've done in a long time. I wasn't sure what I hoped to accomplish here. Seeing Morgan's house, the abandoned hovel I was approaching, seemed like a good idea at the time, but now that I was here, I regretted the decision.

Actually, I regretted it in spades.

The house that stood before me was not one I could ever imagine Morgan living in. Years of decay rotted the wood, and there were so many shingles missing from the slanted roof, I wondered how the damn thing stayed up in the first place. If this monstrosity wasn't smack dab in the center of a prominent residential area, I never would have pegged it for a home anyone might want. It was no wonder the town tried to purchase the property back from the couple that bought it. The thing was an eyesore that was better off being torn down. No way in hell would Morgan, or anyone else, live here.

Checking the surrounding homes, I made sure the neighbors weren't outside before creeping closer to the entrance. The porch floors creaked as I walked, and I tightened the black hood of my sweatshirt around my face. The outfit made me look like some pathetic version of a bank robber out on a job. Whatever. As long as no one saw me sneak inside, I didn't care what I looked like.

My hand grasped the door handle and disappointment crashed through me when it didn't turn. I didn't know why I expected it to be so easy. Maybe because this place looked like a two-story pile of garbage, I simply assumed no one would bother locking it up. Though there was a good chance the town deemed the house a hazard to avoid kids breaking in to party. I seriously hoped the whole thing didn't collapse on me.

After giving the handle another failed try, I considered casting a door opening spell but chose against it. The place was hanging on for dear life and the way my magic has been behaving lately, one wrong move and I could topple it all to the ground. Instead, I pulled the small knife hidden in my boot and slid the tip into the thin slit of the doorframe. The knife was nothing like the dagger Daria stole from me, and I missed my trusty weapon. One of these days, I had to spell another to replace it, but in the meantime, the knife River let me borrow from his collection would have to do. It was small enough to fit into my boot, and tonight, it was exactly what I needed.

Sliding the silver further down, I jiggled the handle until I heard a click and pushed the knife into the lock bracket. One quick twist and the door slid open like butter. Honestly, I was a little impressed with how easy it was to break into this place, though granted, Shadowhurst wasn't ready for the likes of me. I had been breaking into secure locations for years to hunt shadowers, and this was a walk in the park for a criminal such as myself.

Not something to be proud of, Billie. Don't be a creep.

Dropping my smile, I slunk into the opening and closed the door behind me. As soon as I was inside, my heart dropped to my feet. This was Morgan's house. I just knew it.

The mixture of streetlamps and moonlight strobed through the uncovered windows and illuminated enough of the house for me to see. No furniture decorated the space, and the inside was just as gross as the exterior. Old wallpaper hung shredded on the walls, and the distinct scent of mold permeated the house, invading my senses. My eyes stung from the stench, and I coughed into my sleeve before continuing to make my way through the dingy place.

My gaze drifted over every room, hoping to find something that would bring me to Morgan. Each room was emptier than the first, and each one made my nerves spike as I walked through. A lonely fireplace stood in the center of the living room and my heart shattered when I thought about Morgan spending cozy evenings here with her parents. A few doors down, a decrepit kitchen unfolded, bringing only more heartache and regret with it. How many breakfasts had Morgan missed since she'd been gone? How many dinners?

Too many, I decided and turned the corner into a hallway.

I checked more rooms than I could count, and by the time I finished searching the first floor, I was so defeated, I nearly broke down.

"What did you think would happen?" I asked the empty house. "That she'd be here waiting for you? Nice going."

My fingers curled and I pressed my fists to the wall, pounding my forehead into the old wallpaper and making dust rise all around me. It sparkled in the small streams of light and shot up my nose until I had to fight back sneeze after sneeze while my eyes watered. My hair fell over my face, and I pressed my hand to the wall, ready to call it a night.

Suddenly, to my left, a shadow moved, and my head snapped in its direction. My jaw slacked and my eyes widened as I tried to peer into the darkness. There was nothing but an empty hallway and dirty carpet in this spot, but a few feet before me, an enormous staircase unfolded. The wood railing had seen better days and the steps looked as though they might break underfoot, yet that did little to deflect me.

Just above, I saw another shadow shiver and I jerked my gaze to the top landing of the stairs. The house was as eerily quiet as before. Still, something urged me forward. Step by step, I climbed until I reached the second floor and was surrounded by bedrooms. From here, I could see the master suite at the end of the hall, and it looked big enough to rival the entire guesthouse at home. Next to it, another bedroom sat abandoned. Something tugged me to turn around, and when I did, my mouth gaped open.

Before me, another doorway emerged.

The paint was scraped, revealing rotten wood under-neath and a rusty door handle on its side. As I approached, my finger trailed the doorframe, running over the small ridges carved into the wood. They were almost equally spaced out until they reached just above my waist, and I noticed someone had chiseled numbers next to them. I scooted down, pulling a phone from my pants and turning on the flashlight. When the light hit the markings, a gasp escaped my lips and I stumbled back.

In the wood, tiny inscriptions floated next to the slashes, each one with a date and an initial.

M.T.

Morgan Theron.

My breath caught in my throat, and I jumped to my feet, pushing my way into the room. Into *her* room. I was so sure this was it that when I fumbled in, I almost cried seeing it empty again. Actually, I did cry. A LOT. Uncontrollable tears fell down my face, and I choked back sobs while racing around the room. The phone's glow slashed across the walls and floor in lasers, and my eyes searched wildly over every inch of space. I patted the walls, looking for anything of value.

"There's nothing here," I whispered into the dusty air.

Outside, the streetlamps poured light in through the small window. I tip-toed to the sill, perching on it to peer outside. I imagined Morgan sitting here on summer days, listening to music, and watching people pass by outside. Thinking of her, tears blurred my vision, and I grew desperate for fresh air before I passed the hell out. With shaking hands, I reached for the bottom of the window to pull it open when something sliced across my finger.

"Ouch!" I yelped, looking at the slight cut and the blood that dried around it. "What the hell?"

Shaking my hand, I felt the window's ledge again and wrapped my fingers around a piece of paper trapped between the frame and wall. I wiggled it out, and brought it to my face, aiming the phone's light at its center.

"Holy. Freaking. Shit," I cursed as I inspected the paper.

Clutching it with trembling hands, I studied the photograph. It was old enough for the edges to yellow and covered in so much dust, I had to wipe it clean with my thumb.

Despite the shoddy state of the picture, there was no mistaking what I was looking at. There, in my clammy fingers, was a photo of Morgan. Her red hair tied in a loose ponytail and her smile spreading from ear to ear. Next to her, Peyton beamed as she looked at her girlfriend with so much joy, it made my head spin. I was right. Morgan lived in this house, and someone didn't want people to know that. Someone wanted her to disappear.

Chapter
Eleven

Billie

*B*y the time I biked to school, my face was frozen, and my lips chapped from the frigid winds that spelled the upcoming winter. My leather jacket's lining was soaked in a cold sweat and I could feel the ridges of the photograph I tucked in the pocket rub against my chest. For some reason, I couldn't leave Morgan at home today. It seemed between the photograph and the staurolite hidden in my backpack, I was carrying the weight of my imaginary friends everywhere I went. Except Morgan wasn't imaginary and just thinking it made my heart pitter-patter.

Soon, I would find her. There were no other options for me here.

Having opted to be on time this morning, I told River I'll see him at lunch and rode my bike at the break of dawn, taking the longer route through the town. I wanted to swing by the Crystal Cauldron before school, but when I passed by, the shop was still closed and there was no sign of Ms. Broussard. After a few useless knocks, I left and headed for the academy, knowing full well I'd be one of the few students to arrive this early. Not that it bothered me. It was nice to have some peace and quiet to clear my head before everyone else trickled in for class.

Sauntering to first period, I smiled as I passed the rows of lockers lining the corridor. Everything was still such a mess that I rarely let myself feel thankful for where life had taken me. It wasn't so long ago that I was still in the High Coven's clutches, blind as a bat to their evil ways, and following their rules like a good little soldier. Never in my wildest dreams could I have imagined the life I now had in Shadowhurst. This place, this school, had become my sanctuary and I wondered how Beatrix would feel if she knew where her daughter ended up.

Would she be proud of me for going against the coven?

I wasn't sure why I was thinking of my mom right now. Any time she popped into my head, I was usually pretty confused about it. The woman wasn't a stellar role model, yet I still couldn't get her damn memory erased. My thumb rubbed against the empty spot where the moonstone ring once sat, and I frowned. It was just another piece of the puzzle that was my past gone.

I couldn't get a break, could I?

The classroom was empty except for two students when I walked in, and I took the free time before class started to study Morgan's photograph further. Despite trying to sleep, I stayed up all night looking at it, and at this point, I could probably count all the hunter's freckles with my eyes closed. *I'll find you. I promise I will find you soon.*

A throat cleared beside me, and I shoved the picture under my notebook before looking up.

"What's that?" Peyton asked, her voice loud enough to make the other students turn around.

So much for peace and quiet...

I pressed my hands to the notebook protectively. "Just an old picture I found in the guest house. Nothing important."

To my relief, Peyton relaxed and slumped down into her seat.

"You're here early," I noted. "That's a first."

"Ugh," she sighed, slouching. Her purple sneaker kicked a table leg, and she rattled a berry-tinted nail against the wood. "My stupid dad is literally all over me these days. 'Do your homework. Eat your vegetables. Go to school on time.' Like chill, dude. It's so annoying."

"Doesn't he know you at all?" I chuckled.

"Right? You'd think seventeen years in, and he suddenly forgot who he was dealing with. I don't do *on time*."

"Yet, here you are..."

She scowled, narrowing her eyes on me. "Don't mess with me, B. I've only had one cup of coffee and it won't be pretty."

Letting out another giggle, I shifted in my seat to face her. My hands shook and I shoved them under my legs to keep steady. That morning, I decided to ask Peyton for help to figure out the Morgan situation without revealing what I knew, but now that it was time to do so, I was a ball of nerves. *Rip off the Band-Aid. She's your best friend; what are you so scared of?* Taking a deep breath in, I locked my eyes on Peyton. "Hey, think you could help me with something?"

"Sure thing, girl. What's up?"

"I, uh, I was hoping you might be into helping me figure out this whole me imagining a person thing."

Peyton's face paled and she bit the inside of her cheek. "I thought River said you were fine now?"

"I am!" I exclaimed. "Definitely. But it got me thinking. When Vic said the High Coven was up to something, I got worried. What if they're working on some spell we don't know about and this is the aftermath or something? There's so much the high priestesses keep to themselves that I'm scared this is a part of it."

"Okay, but isn't Vic working on that?"

"She is, yeah." *How do I do this?* "Except Vic is working on the fae side of things. I was thinking you and I can hit the magic part. Maybe team up with Ms. Broussard and see if we can dig up a spell that might have a side effect like this. It could be worth a shot."

Peyton looked skeptical and my chest constricted when I thought about her telling the rest of our friends I was still a freaking loon. This was a bad idea. I should have left her out of it and worked on solving the whole thing myself. Now, River would for sure be glued to my side twenty-four seven. What an absolute disaster.

Why don't I ever think these things through?

"You definitely think a spell can do this?" Peyton asked, and my eyes widened. "Like something to make you imagine a whole flipping person?!? That's wild, B. Even for the coven."

A smile tugged at my lips as the tension in my back gave way and I leaned across the table to get closer to her. "There's a spell for pretty much everything."

"Cool shit, girl!"

Inching closer, I glanced around the class as though to make sure we weren't overheard. Of course, no one cared, but I knew if there was mystery afoot, my best friend would be on it like a truffle pig. When I saw Peyton's mouth drop open, I knew I had her hooked. "This could be dangerous," I croaked out. "It's magic I don't even understand."

"Girl, please," Peyton said. "You had me at spell."

Laughing, I slumped in my seat and watched a few more students drag their tired bodies into the classroom. Two girls giggled hysterically as they marched past us, not offering so much as a hello. It didn't bother me one bit. I was so used to sticking to the shadows. It was actually a preferable way to exist as far as I was concerned. You'd think dating River would have made me more popular at this school, but that wasn't the case at all. Guess that went to show you, once invisible, always invisible. Considering I was a witch dating a witch hunter and hanging out with a bunch of shadowers after school, invisible was exactly how I needed to stay.

"So, what's the plan?" Peyton asked, tearing my attention away from the girls.

"Don't have one," I admitted. "That's kind of why I need your help."

My best friend cracked her knuckles and flipped a strand of hair off her face. "Don't have to ask me twice," she announced. "Here's what I'm thinking. We gotta start at the Crystal Cauldron, for sure. Bring your grimoire and ask Vic for the Book of Darkness. Or at least ask her to be on standby in case we call with questions. We also need Lorelei."

"I knew you're the right woman for the job!" I teased, bumping her shoulder. "Why Lorelei, though?"

"Amateurs," Peyton said, letting go of an exasperated sigh that told me she was over me. "If this is a spell, then it's all about mind control. Who else do we know that has the power to fuck with someone's head like that?"

"Oh... my..."

"Peyton. *Oh, my Peyton* is what you're looking for." She smirked before continuing. "Shadower magic is part witch magic, right? Since they like made us or whatever."

I nodded.

"Okay, then mind reapers probably got their power from witch magic of some kind. Something inside your kind's magic triggered their mind control anomaly. Vic should still keep looking into the fae though. We need that too."

"You think this is both fae and witch related?"

"Obvi. One led to the other, right?"

Damn. She was good. I didn't even think about that part. If there was a spell out there that could make everyone in Shadowhurst forget Morgan, it had to be powerful enough to screw with an entire town. That had original witch written all over it.

For the first time, I felt hopeful. With Peyton's quick thinking, and mine and Vic's knowledge of spellwork, we actually stood a chance at figuring this out. All I had to do was make certain no one suspected I still believed Morgan was real and I'd be golden.

"Thanks for helping," I told Peyton with a smile.

"Are you kidding? Anything to get me away from dad and his prison warden attitude. You know he's already on my ass to look at colleges?"

While Peyton continued to recount all the ways her dad annoyed her on the daily, I let my mind wander. This was a step in the right direction, an entire leap, in fact. I was going to find that spell and use it to lead me to the asshole who cast it. I had the sense the High Coven had something to do with this, and with Peyton's help, I could find out how and why they did this. Those witches were going down and I wouldn't rest until they did. And, on the off chance we discovered the fae were involved—a very big if since no one's seen one of them in decades—I would deal with them too. There was no way in Hell would I let anyone mess with my friends and get away with it.

Fae or witch, whoever took Morgan from our lives was going to pay. They were going to pay hard.

Chapter Twelve

River

*C*ool air blasted around my face and pushed ripples across the small pond at the back of the school while Savannah and I reclined in the dry grass. Although, with summer officially over, it was more dirt than grass and I could see my best friend frown as she dusted fresh stains from her pants.

"This is disgusting," she announced, rising to stand. "Why did we think it was a good idea to chill here?"

"Because we always come here after school," I answered. "At least we used to."

She scoffed, patting at another patch of dirt on her light blue jeans. "Well, we were idiots then. This place is gross."

Laughing, I rested my hands on my knees and stretched my legs out. My own pants were equally covered in crap, and I had to admit, it wasn't the best look. But I missed hanging out with Savannah, so when Billie said she was spending time with Peyton after school, I took it as a sign. I probably should have thought this out a little better. Coming to this pond had been mine and Sav's favorite thing to do since we

75

started high school, and I guess I just assumed it would make me feel better to relive old times.

Judging by her disturbed face, my plan failed miserably.

"Stop being a baby and chill out," I said.

"Easy for you to say," she snapped back. "Not all of us have a ball and chain. Some people still have to look presentable, you know."

"Wow! Easy. And Billie's not a ball and chain."

"Yeah, yeah. Whatever." Savannah shrugged, lowering to crouch inches from the ground. "Got anything on your stupid mate bond yet?"

She meant no harm with the question, yet it still sent shivers down my spine. I let it hang in the air for a few moments before finally relaxing and letting the anger subside. A little.

"Nope," I answered. "The lines haven't come back since we got Billie out of that cave. I'm worried they're gone for good."

"That's stupid, even for you."

My jaw tensed. "Are you basically here to mock me or do you have something good to say?"

"All I'm saying is that if it's the bond like you think it is, I doubt it can go away. I mean, look at Mel and Raiden. It has those two tied at the hip. It's nauseating."

"Yeah, but they have an actual mate bond. I don't even know what this thing that happened to me and Billie is. It was there when she was in trouble, and then it was just gone. Maybe she's right and I'm overthinking it. It's probably a fluke and I'm so desperate for it to be the bond, I let myself get carried away."

"Or it *is* the bond and you need to calm the hell down."

Savannah grinned and I frowned.

"God, you really don't get girls at all, do you?"

Bewildered, I looked my best friend up and down. *What on earth is this girl getting at now?*

"Huh?"

Savannah's nose wrinkled and she looked away from me to the rippling pond at our feet. The curls of her hair spun in the wind, tossing and turning over her head. She reminded me of a modern-day Medusa, and I seriously waited for snakes to peer back at me when she turned. Instead, Savannah brushed the unruly mane away and settled to sit, a disgruntled look on her face. Considering everything that happened between us, I couldn't imagine being this close to any of our other friends. It was always me and Sav against the world until Billie came along. That couldn't have been easy for her, but I had to hand it to Savannah, she was handling it like a champ.

Billie was right. Savannah was tough as nails, and I was proud to call her my best friend.

After a long moment of silence, Savannah looked at me. "Billie's been through some shit."

"I know that. What does that have to do with any of this?"

"Like I said," she said, shaking her head, "totally clueless. Your little bond thingie is all about emotions, right? It's the strongest form of connection you could have with another person?"

"Uh-huh..."

"Okay. And Billie's emotions are all over the place, yeah?"

"Yep..."

Savannah patted my shoulder in pity and half-smiled. "Don't you think there's a chance that you can't feel her through whatever those weird-ass lines were until she's done freaking out?"

I considered it for a second, then shook my head.

"I don't know. She was freaking out in that cave, and I had no problem connecting to her then."

"Then is not now," Savannah said harshly. "Mel told me everyone's mate bond snaps into place in different ways, but it always happens when two people are on the same emotional wavelength. It's like some supernatural consent form or something. Super weird."

"Wait, you asked Mel about this?"

Savannah grinned. "Obvi. You were worried, so was Billie. Someone had to be the adult here and figure some shit out."

A loud laugh escaped me, and I bumped her shoulder with my own. "You know, if you keep talking smack, I might wolf out on you."

"I'd like to see you try, Cujo," she snapped.

"Still not a thing."

I could see the attitude in her change as she started to argue, but something else caught my eyes in the distance. My back tensed and my jaw ticked as I watched a familiar shape scurry down the hill toward us. The blood in my veins pulsed no matter how hard I tried to bottle up my emotions. As Logan neared us, something inside told me to stay alert. Why was I still so mistrustful of the guy? He had done nothing but have our backs time and time again, and yet, I couldn't bring myself to relax around him. Something about the mind reaper rubbed me the wrong way like he was a puzzle I couldn't figure out. It was no surprise. Despite the time Savannah had been spending with him, there was very little we knew about Logan. He appeared out of nowhere, and in my experience, that was never a good thing.

"Some school you got here, chaps," Logan said when he approached us, his British accent rolling off his tongue like honey. "Not too shabby at all."

"Don't be dense," Savannah hissed. "It's a freaking school. Get over it."

"Get over it? That's a bloody pond over there!" Logan crouched by the water, running his hand through the stream and wiping it on his ripped denim pants. "The other half sure knows how to have a good time, don't they?"

Savannah sighed and threw a small rock at his head, which Logan dodged easily. "First time you see water, huh?" she joked. "It's this wonderful invention some of us use for showering. Try it sometime."

Logan's lips curled at the edges, and it shocked me to see him entertained by Savannah's attitude. If it was me, I would have been arguing with her already, but not Logan. He was amused. Almost as though he liked the shade she was throwing his way. *Interesting.*

"You know, back where I'm from," Logan said, "ponds like these were scarce. You're pretty lucky, princess."

My ears perked up. "Where *are* you from by the way?"

"Here and there," Logan said, answering absolutely nothing at all. "Nowhere you'd be able to point out on a map."

"That's because they don't put trash bins on a map," Savannah bit back.

Logan laughed so loud, my eardrums vibrated.

"You're not wrong about that, princess," he said, shadows growing behind his eyes. "Ready to go?"

Savannah sighed and rose to stand. "Just don't talk until we get there, okay?"

"You're leaving?" I asked. The tension in my spine returned and I found myself not wanting to let my best friend go. I wanted to think it was because I was being a child who wanted his friend to himself, but that wasn't it. I didn't like her around Logan. I didn't like it in the least.

"We're going to the house. Train some more. You should come!" Savannah offered.

I thought about it. I really, really did. Getting away from my racing mind was a good plan, and I definitely needed to train. Fighting was something I cherished since I was a kid, and it was the one thing that kept me grounded. Even after finding out my mother pushed me into witch hunting, I never once despised her for it. It taught me how to handle myself and how to have control. A thing I very much needed. Still, I didn't want to be back at the resistance. Not with the pack so close by and my wolf going bonkers every time other shifters were around. Besides, I had to stay close in case Billie needed me.

I was seriously pathetic.

Inside, the wolf agreed and I tried not to hate him for it. Pathetic or not, she was my top priority, and everything had to take a backseat. Even my best friend.

"Next time," I told Savannah. "You two have fun."

Logan wiggled his eyebrows and Sav slapped his shoulder, pushing past him to leave. As they disappeared over the hill, leaving me alone, I watched them retreat and the turmoil in my chest intensified. I couldn't get over how odd I felt around Logan. My mind raced as I tried to think of anything that might explain it, but came up empty. Logan was a stranger, and that stranger was getting awfully friendly with my best friend. I had to find out more about him, if not for any other reason than to be certain Savannah was safe to spend time with the reaper.

One more thing to add to the list, I thought, lying back down. *Save Billie from herself. Figure out what's up with the mate bond. Dig into Logan's past. No problem. No freaking problem at all.*

Chapter Thirteen

Billie

"Hurry up, B!" Peyton yelled over her shoulder and darted through the trees.

My breath caught in my throat as I chased my best friend down the narrow path in the woods leading to the resistance. Leaves crunched underfoot and the smell of pine rushed up to my nostrils with each step closer to the house. Having decided to pick up Lorelei on our way to the Crystal Cauldron, my excitement for figuring out what the hell was going on in Shadowhurst bubbled to the surface as I followed Peyton through the forest.

In the distance, I could see the house rise on the horizon, and a smile tugged at the corners of my mouth. We were so close to answers, I could almost taste it.

Peyton jogged up the stairs, not bothering to knock before entering. This place was as much hers now as anyone else's since she took on a leadership role with the resistance. It was odd to see my friend act with so much superiority, but I had to admit, cockiness fit Peyton like a glove. This girl was built to tell people what to do, and it pleased me to see her content with her new position.

As soon as we walked in, I could tell something was wrong.

Shouts drifted down the tight hallway that opened up to the rest of the house, and Peyton and I exchanged uneasy glances before following their direction. The walls shook from something crashing in a distant room, and we pumped our legs to run faster.

When we reached it, my jaw hit the floor.

Four wolves stood in the center, their eyes glowing and their jaws dripping wet with saliva. Surrounding them, two leopards and a mid-sized bear snarled, burying their paws into the rackety wood floors and crushing it to splinters. The air was so thick, it made the top of my mouth feel slimy and my pulse raced as I turned to my best friend.

"What the..."

Peyton stepped in front of me to face the angry shifters. "Stop this shit right now!"

The leopards cast a sideways glance her way but didn't back down. Next to them, the bear only growled and moved closer to the wolves huddling in the center. At its approach, one wolf pushed off the floor and leaped forward, sinking its teeth into the bear's matted mess of brown fur. A loud howl pierced the room as the remaining wolves jumped to attack, and my heart shot up my throat.

Without thinking, I broke into a dead sprint and was smack-dab in the center of the madness in seconds. Not far from me, Peyton followed suit and before we knew it, a fight broke out around us. Growls and yelps pierced the air, and I struggled to tell one shifter from the next. There was so much chaos, I couldn't keep my eyes focused.

A flash of grey fur zoomed in my peripheral vision, and I twirled on my heels just in time to avoid getting trampled by a wolf. It lunged past me, zeroing in on a leopard and pushing it down with massive paws. The leopard twisted under the wolf's weight, scrambling to get free. It was too slow. The wolf dug its canines into the leopard's throat and a painful cry ripped through the room.

My eyes widened and I froze in my spot. *This isn't normal.*

There was so much anger surrounding me that my brain hurt when I tried to think of the best way to get everyone to calm the hell down before things ended badly. Near to me, I could see Peyton come to the same conclusion, panic spreading over her face.

"Get those two," she said, nudging her head to the two shifters closest to me. "I'll get the others."

She didn't have to tell me twice.

In a flash, I rounded on the bear and pounced on its wide back, wrapping my arms around what I hoped was a neck. The beast was so large, it was hard to tell which part was which, but when I finally got a grip, I could sense its surprise under my hold. The bear pulled back from the wolf trapped under its weight, giving the animal just enough time to scramble away. Then it shook its gargantuan body. My head rattled as the bear fought to throw me off, and I clutched my fingers around clumps of fur to stay atop it.

"Use your magic!" Peyton shouted.

I started to obey her call and paused. Memories of my destroyed room flashed before me, and I almost lost my grip on the bear.

"I can't!" I yelled back. "I don't want to hurt them!"

On my left, Peyton shook her head and stretched her

arms out. One step was all it took for her to touch one wolf, and the poor creature was on the floor in seconds. Its body convulsed as Peyton's power drove through it, rendering the animal unconscious. When the wolf was down, my best friend twisted around to the leopards. Their spotted furs rippled as their thick bodies hit the ground, shivering lightly. Their eyes rolled back into their heads, and I saw Peyton drop beside them to make sure they were still breathing. When she was satisfied, she moved on to the wolf behind her.

Beneath me, the bear grunted and slid backward, hitting the wall with me still strapped to its back. The breath knocked out of me and my hold on its fur lessened, dropping me to the floor like a sack of crap. A dull pain ran up my spine and I rubbed my neck to loosen the tension. As I did, the bear turned, its jaw wide open and ready to tear me to pieces.

Loud footsteps thundered in the doorway, and I glimpsed Raiden and Mel charging into the room just as the bear lunged for me. Sliding my ass across the floorboards, I twirled out of its way, landing on all fours behind it. The bear's giant head hit the wall and it growled in anger before turning around to face me again.

"Screw this!" I screamed and reached for my magic.

I wanted the shadows. I wanted them so badly, I could scream. Instead, when my hands shot out, a new sensation flooded my system. My fingers tingled and a blazing heat tore through me. Before me, the bear whimpered, its eyes widening in horror as it watched my magic unfurl. Smoke rose from my fingers and my chest tightened as small sparks appeared under the surface of my skin. The tips of my fingers glowed bright red, and I took in ragged breaths with each hit of magic that rushed through me. When more smoke flowed from my hands, the heat intensified until I could barely stand it. It felt as though my entire body was on fire.

Not knowing what to do, I balled up my hands into fists and forced my arms to my sides. Whatever magic I was about to unleash was not something I wanted to mess with. It felt foreign and unchartered and unlike any energy I have felt before. *What was that?* I had no clue, and I wasn't about to find out. This wasn't the shadow magic I possessed, it wasn't even the elemental magic I wielded in the cavern or my room earlier that week. Whatever energy was coursing through me now was new, and this was not the right time to use it. The bear shifter didn't deserve to end up on the wrong end of my unruly magic.

"Get out of the way!" Raiden called out behind me.

I swerved to the side, giving the fridge-sized man a wide berth as he rushed by me to pin the bear to the wall. Raiden's thick fingers tightened around the shifter's neck, and he let out a low growl. His eyes narrowed when he faced the bear dead on. "Shift back now," Raiden hissed. "I won't ask again."

The bear snapped its jaw but obeyed. Its bones cracked and its limbs shot out to the sides as he reformed. I had only a moment to blink; when I looked up, a man hung limp in Raiden's hold. His eyes were apologetic like he was a child scolded for eating too much sugar and not a giant shifter that almost killed people.

"They started it," the man said in between breaths.

I followed his gaze to the wolves, who were all in their human form now. On the opposite end of the room, the leopards were still in their animal shapes and passed out on the floor. *What an actual shit show.*

Raiden uncurled his fingers from the man's throat. To my right, Mel loosened her grip on the wolf shifter she held down, coming to stand next to Peyton.

"What even happened here?" I asked, still baffled by what I witnessed.

Raiden's brow creased and he looked around the room. "The wolves have been having a hard time without an alpha."

"That's what we're calling this?" Peyton asked. "A hard time? Seriously?"

I had so many questions, I didn't even know where to start.

"Is this not the first time it happened?" I asked, hoping someone would explain what the heck was going on. I hadn't been gone for that long, yet it seemed everything was different in the house. *Why did no one tell me this?* I wondered if River knew about it, and if he did, why he wouldn't offer the information. Unless he was protecting me somehow. The thought alone made me so angry, I had to shove my hands in my pockets to keep from punching walls. Or shifters. Neither one was a good idea, so instead, I bit the inside of my cheek and kept my eyes on Raiden while I waited for him to explain.

The lion shifter glanced from Mel to me. "We've had some issues lately, nothing to worry about. Once the wolves have an alpha again, it will be fine. They're a rowdy bunch, so fights are inevitable."

"You're just letting this slide?" I asked, baffled. "They could have killed each other!"

"We're not letting anything slide," Mel interjected.

"And what do you call this?"

"Comes with the territory," she said. "Shifters are not

like other shadowers. We have primal needs and unfortunately, we tend to solve our problems physically."

Were these people for real right now? They were acting as though these idiots had no say in the matter. Like they couldn't control their own emotions unless they were pounding each other to dust. Worry set in the base of my stomach. *Is River the same?*

I was about to ask more questions when a bright flash of blue tore my attention from the room and landed on the small window opposite us. It was so quick, I wasn't sure I even saw it at all. Judging by the nonchalant expressions on everyone's face, I was the only one that noticed the disturbance.

"What was that?" I asked, looking around the room. "Anyone see that light?"

They shook their heads, making me feel crazy all over again.

"Guys, come on," I urged. "No one else saw that just now?"

Greeted with more confused faces, I let it drop. I was probably still shaken up from when that stupid bear shoved me into the wall, and knowing my luck, had a nice concussion to remember the whole event by. Rubbing the back of my head, I let my gaze drift to Peyton, eager to get out of the damn house and back to our initial plan. If the shifters wanted to beat each other senseless, it was their problem. It wasn't my place to tell these morons what to do.

"Whatever," I hissed. "Let's get Lorelei and head to the Crystal Cauldron. I'm over this place."

The room grew silent, and Peyton's eyebrows kissed when she looked at me.

"Um, B? What are you talking about?"

I sighed. "I'm saying I don't want to deal with this crap right now. Grab Lorelei. I don't want to keep Vic waiting long. We have bigger things to worry about than these guys acting like fools."

Raiden and Mel exchanged worried glances and the shifters in the room mimicked their motion. Beside me, Peyton rested a small hand on my shoulder, whipping me around to face her. Her face grew ashen, and her voice was soft and calculated when she spoke again.

"Girl, who's Lorelei?"

Chapter Fourteen

Billie

This isn't happening. This isn't happening. This isn't happening.

I recited the words the entire time Peyton swerved her Jeep like a maniac on our way to the Crystal Cauldron. Every once in a while, she turned to look at me and I refused to meet her gaze. Keeping my head trained on the passenger side window, I watched the streets blur past as we sped through town and tried to avoid the concerned stares my best friend shot my way. Not that I could blame her for worrying. As far as Peyton was concerned, I was making up an entirely new person. Again.

This time though, when I realized what happened, I was smarter.

Instead of trying to convince everyone that Lorelei vanished, something I knew would make me look insane yet again, I simply told them I hit my head and switched the subject. It was easy enough to get my friends off the topic since no one but me remembered Lorelei in the first place.

Though I could tell Peyton wasn't on board with my performance. My best friend could see right through me and even back at the house, I knew this wasn't something she would let slide. But hey, I had to at least try to look normal. No point repeating the same mistake I made with Morgan, especially now that I knew I wasn't imagining the entire thing.

We didn't stay long at the resistance before I urged Peyton to leave, telling her that Vic and Ms. Broussard were waiting for us. There was no point in searching the house for any trace of Lorelei. I had already learned that lesson with Morgan. Whatever made the mind reaper disappear would not leave any clues. My best bet was to stick to the plan and find the spell that caused all this. It was the only way to bring Morgan and Lorelei back.

And yet, I still couldn't quite believe this was happening all over again.

This town is the actual freaking worst.

Peyton stomped on the breaks and my chest flew forward, catching in the seatbelt with a sharp yank. A cough caught in my throat, and I snapped to attention, realizing she had parked us in front of the small occult shop. Outside, Main Street wasn't as busy as it often was on a weekend, and it surprised me not to see crowds of people zoom by. With the colder weather settling in, tourist season was winding down, though Peyton assured me the first hint of snow would bring them right back again. I really wasn't looking forward to that. The seldom quiet days Shadowhurst offered were a blessing. They gave me time to think.

Which was exactly what I was doing when Peyton smacked my arm hard enough to sting.

"Did you hear anything I just said?" she asked, her shoulders high enough to touch her ears.

I grimaced. "Sorry. Space case over here."

"Yeah, no shit. What's up with you? Maybe we should go to the hospital, get your head checked from that hit you took."

"I'm fine," I said. "Let's go in. They're waiting for us."

Reluctantly, my best friend hopped out of the car, and we headed into the shop. The familiar smell of dried herbs penetrated my senses, and I couldn't help but smile as we walked down the narrow store to the front counter. All around me, crystals and greenery lined the shelves and I found myself reaching for their elements. The energies were faint, so faint in fact that I could barely feel them, and it made my stomach turn. This was too similar to when I tried casting the spell in my room. All the pieces were there, but for some reason, I couldn't tap into them. Inside, my magic stayed still and dormant and I wondered why I was having so much trouble connecting to it now. I truly thought after the crap I pulled in the cavern, I'd be stronger. Instead, I was a hot mess. It was as though my magic didn't answer to me anymore and instead, did whatever it wanted whenever it wanted to. Even the shadows refused to come out to play, which was seriously unusual for them. I never realized how much I relied on their energy to keep me going. I mean, those buggers saved my ass on more than one occasion, and I had gotten pretty used to having them around.

I should probably talk to someone about this. The thought was brief, and I shook it off before I could lend it any weight. With everyone concerned about the state of my sanity, the last thing I needed was to add fuel to the fire. There was no reason to worry them further. *Find the spell, get your friends back, then figure out your magic. Good plan.*

"Finally!" a shrill voice shot toward us. I tore my eyes off the shelves to see Vic's head poking up from behind the glass counter. Her obsidian hair was tied into a staple high ponytail and her inky eyes sparkled as she watched us walk over. Vic's eyebrows arched and she half-smiled in that sneaky way she often did when she had something to share. "You won't believe what I found!"

So predictable.

Stepping closer to the counter, I peered past Vic's shoulder to the books scattered on the floor. There were at least ten tomes spread out at her feet, and I vaguely recognized several of them. From the looks of it, Vic had made herself quite at home in the shop and I wondered how Ms. Broussard handled having the feisty witch around. As far as I could tell, she had kept the Crystal Cauldron nice and tidy, and seeing Vic go to town on the books made me cringe. The girl was as messy as they came.

"Where's Ms. Broussard?" I asked, looking around the shop.

"Getting tea, or something like that," Vic answered, uninterested in the shop owner's whereabouts. "Not the point. You have got to see this!"

Peyton nudged my side just as Vic plopped the Book of Darkness on the counter. The weight of the grimoire bounced off the glass and made every display atop rattle from the impact. I caught a large amethyst point before it fell off the edge and took a deep breath in relief. Setting the crystal back on the counter, I leaned over to see what Vic pointed to. Her finger tapped at one page in particular. It was a spell I hadn't noticed in the book before. As I read over the instructions, confusion set in, and I let my lips part in awe.

"This is the same spell Evanora used to drain fae energy from the students," I said.

At my words, Peyton's eyes narrowed, and she turned the book to face her. Her knuckles rattled against the glass counter while she read, and I could see the wheels in her head turning. When she finished, Peyton looked up at me, bewildered. "Why is this spell in here? Isn't this your family's grimoire?"

"I don't have a family," I said sternly.

"I meant that Graves wrote this book, and she's part of your family line of witches, right?"

I nodded. "How much do you know about Evanora, Vic?"

"River filled me in," my friend said with a grin. "And this is definitely the spell she used to suck up fae powers."

"Why would an original witch bother creating this spell in the first place?" Peyton asked. "Didn't they get all their magic from the fae? I get that Evanora wanted to become more powerful, but it doesn't make sense for an original witch to do this. Like those chicks had access to fae magic any time they wanted it. I don't get it."

Vic's cheeks flushed and she tore the book from Peyton to flip through the pages again. "I haven't figured that out yet, but I found this too." She pointed to another entry in the grimoire. This one was only a few sentences long and seemed to have been written as an afterthought. "'Our time has come'," Vic read aloud. "'We shall rise and take our rightful place in this world, and all those before us shall be deleted. Their memory will haunt us no longer'."

My jaw tensed and I reached for Peyton's hand, tangling our fingers together.

"What does that mean? Is there anything else after?"

Shaking her head, Vic's gaze found mine and she leaned in across the counter. "This was all I found so far that sounded even remotely close to what we're looking for. I don't think you're crazy, Billie. I think Graves knew how to erase someone from existence and that whoever is messing with this town found it out too. If I'm right, there's original magic at play here."

"So, what does that mean?" Peyton asked.

"That we're in deep shit," I answered. "And so is everyone else in Shadowhurst."

Clutching the Book of Darkness to my chest, I walked down the winding suburban street leading me home. By the time I left the Crystal Cauldron, the sun had set and darkness settled over town in a blanket of silence. Peyton offered to drive me home, but I refused. After what Vic found out, I needed to clear my head, and walking did just that. My thoughts raced as I made my way toward the Chandler residence, eager to get home and tell River what we discovered. I probably should have called before I left the shop, but with my head all over the place, it seemed a better idea to collect myself first.

I was still trying to wrap my mind around the fact that Graves was an ancestor of mine and an original witch to boot. Adding the spell and ominous note Vic found in the grimoire didn't help at all. Something continued to tug at the back of my brain, and I couldn't seem to grasp it. It was as though the answer was right there, waiting for me to find it. Yet, I couldn't see anything at all. Why was the spell

Evanora used in the book? And what did all of this have to do with Morgan and Lorelei?

The more I thought about it, the more questions I had, until my temples pounded and the knots in my stomach tightened enough to make me want to puke.

At least Vic believes you now. Maybe Peyton, too.

The idea offered little solace. Even if I had people on my side that didn't think I was totally crazy, and that was still a big 'if' at this point, it didn't get me any closer to finding out what happened to my friends. Or who did this to them? There were too many pieces missing, and without them, I had no chance of getting to the bottom of this mess.

What if I don't figure it out and someone else gets erased?

My vision blurred and I shook the thought off before it could do more damage. I couldn't lose hope, not now. Tightening my grasp on the book, I took in a deep breath and let it out. This damn grimoire had the answers, I only had to find them.

Behind me, dry leaves rustled, and I stopped in my tracks.

My fingers wrapped around the leather spine of the grimoire and butterflies danced in my gut when I felt eyes on my back. Next to me, a shadow crept over the pavement, growing as whoever followed me approached. My shoulders stiffened, creeping up to meet my ears. Steadily, I twisted on my heels and turned around, blood draining from my face in an instant. Moonlight illuminated most of the street, drawing eerie shadows across the features of the tall head witch that stood before me. Her sinister grin widened, and she thrust her arms outward, magic dancing on the tips of her fingers. I had no time to react. Before I could move, the surge of her magic exploded and barreled straight for my face, hurdling through the air with a speed so fast, it was sure to strike me dead.

I swerved right, losing my grip on the grimoire and sending it flying from my hands. It landed a few feet away with a thud, drawing the attention of the head witch that attacked me. We dove for the book in unison, me reaching it first with only seconds to spare. *So, this is what you're after.*

The head witch's eyes darkened as she got ready for another attack. Before she could follow through, I tossed the book into the thick wall of shrubbery near to me and reached for my magic.

Considering how things have been going, there was a good chance I would kill this woman with my power, but I couldn't care less. It was a chance I was willing to take to protect the grimoire.

I searched for my magic, urging for its energy to burst from me right that instant. When nothing happened, I closed my eyes and tried again. Deep down, I could feel the shadows rile, yet something held them back. Nausea crept up my throat and I attempted to reach the other elements around me. My first instinct was to search for the earth's energy since I seemed to have had no trouble connecting to it in the cavern. Placing my hands on the ground, I prayed to the Goddess for strength, but she refused to heed my call. My body trembled and the hairs on my neck stood on edge as I switched direction, shooting my arms above me to command the air. It rippled over my head lightly, as if laughing at my incompetence, then stilled again.

Why am I so damn USELESS?!?

A blast of wind crashed into my chest and knocked me backward. My ass hit the pavement as the air burst from my lungs in a white puffy cloud. Eyes unfocused, I fought to get up without success. The head witch let out a cackle and shot another wave of magic at my chest. Twisting on the ground, I got out of its way and scrambled away from her. My attention glued to her face while I reached for the knife in my boot with shaking hands.

Curling my fingers around the handle, I calculated the distance between myself and the witch. *Close enough.*

Without another thought, I flung the knife at the head witch and held my breath. The silver cut the air with a whoosh.

My eyes grew to double size as I watched the knife's tip pierce the witch's flesh just above her heart. She fell backward, screaming from the pain while attempting to rip the knife out. Not bothering to see if she succeeded, I dove for the bushes and dug out the book. I could still hear her crying out behind me while I ran, legs pumping faster with each step. Another pulse of magic rushed by my head, and I turned right, ducking into someone's front yard to get away from the road and the witch's line of sight. As I put more distance between us, her screams died down and I let myself relax.

Taking to the shadows, I took off in a dead sprint until I reached home and collapsed on the front porch. Head jerking from side to side, I made sure the coast was clear before pulling out my cellphone to dial River. The line rang two times before he picked up, and I gasped in relief when I heard his voice.

"Billie?" River asked, his concern filling the phone line.

I didn't bother waiting for him to say anything else. "Can you come over? It's important," I choked out.

"Be there in twenty."

When River hung up, I cradled the Book of Darkness

closer to my heart and gathered myself into a tight ball. That head witch wanted this grimoire, which could only mean one thing. I was right. The High Coven was behind all this, and for some reason, they needed the book. Worse, they were willing to kill me to get it.

Chapter Fifteen

River

My dad would have definitely torn me a new one if he saw how I was driving that night. Not that it mattered much what he thought. Billie needed me, and I was damn sure going to get to her place as fast as possible. By the time I parked the car and made my way to the guesthouse, over twenty minutes have passed and the knot in my stomach had turned entirely solid.

Billie's pale face when she opened the door did not help at all.

"What happened?" I asked, pushing my way inside and inspecting her small apartment. Nothing was out of place, and there was no sign of a struggle. I let my shoulders drop a few inches. "I got here as fast as I could."

Her small hands reached around my neck, and she pulled me in, brushing soft lips against mine. The smell of her skin encircled me, and I could sense the wolf awaken when he felt her nearby. The one thing me and my beast had in common was how much we cared for Billie. Well, that and we were both stubborn as hell.

When Billie pulled away, I had to fight the urge not to kiss her again. *Time and place. Don't be a tool.*

"Are you okay? When you called, it sounded urgent," I managed to blurt out.

Excellent start, Romeo.

"I'm fine now," Billie whispered, and her gaze dropped to my shoes. "A head witch attacked me on the way home. I think she wanted the Book of Darkness."

"WHAT?!?"

She jumped, startled by my outrage.

"I got away," she said, her tone frustrated. "Clearly."

"Babe, I told you to be careful. Why didn't Peyton take you home? Or you could have called me, and I would've grabbed you."

Billie gritted her teeth and her neck reddened. "I don't need babysitters. I wanted to walk and clear my head after what Vic showed us. Running into the witch was a coincidence, but I won't apologize for needing some personal space."

"Babe, no one is saying—" I paused. "Wait, what did Vic show you?"

"Um, well..." Billie hesitated and my breath quickened. Something was going on, and it worried her to tell me. Not that I could blame her, I've been way over the top with keeping tabs on her lately, but it was absolutely necessary. At least, that's what I'd been telling myself.

I squared my shoulders and ran a finger over the soft strands of hair framing her face. "Come on. Spill it."

"Ugh, fine!" She slapped her hands to her thighs. "Vic found the spell your mom used to drain energy from the students in the Book of Darkness. She's convinced my family is somehow connected to it all. That the spell is in the grimoire because Graves wrote it. We still have no idea why an original witch needed a spell like that, in case that's your next question."

"That's what you were worried to tell me?" I asked, with a teasing grin. "I thought something was seriously wrong."

"It is!" Billie exclaimed. "I don't know anything about the witch that supposedly sired my entire freaking family, and this only leads to more questions. Why would she need this spell, River? Why did she need to drain fae energy when she could simply ask the damn fae to give her more power? I don't get any of it!"

Resting a palm on the back of her neck, I traced a circle over her soft skin and felt her relax into me. The nerves building up in her body were palpable and my heart broke thinking of what she must have been going through. I mean, sure, my family history was tainted as shit, but at least I knew what that history was. Except for the whole shapeshifter father thing. That was a bomb my mom dropped I wished I never found out. Granted, if I didn't, my first shift would have been an interesting experience.

I gave Billie's neck a light squeeze and found her eyes. "I know it seems confusing, but we'll get some answers soon. For now, unless it has something to do with how you've been feeling lately, I think it's best to bank the spell you guys found. Concentrate on what's urgent, you know?"

"Yeah, about that..." Billie gasped out, making me weary again. "Vic also found notes in the book that might prove I'm not crazy. There *is* a way to erase someone from memory. We think."

Not this shit again! I really thought we were past this and moving in the right direction. Yet here she was, insisting that the girl she made up was real. I seriously wanted to shake

Billie into clarity. Why couldn't she let this go? Morgan didn't exist, and for some reason, my girl refused to come to her senses. The entire situation was frustrating. I had no clue what to say or do next.

Sensing my discomfort, Billie tilted her head and eyed me up and down. "I'm not crazy, River. I know it, and Vic believes me. Why can't you?"

Because I'm worried you might be crazy after all. Because I can't help you.

"I don't know," I whispered. "It just seems unreal."

Billie threw her head back and laughed.

I glowered.

"Listen, hunter," she said, a ghost of a smile playing on her lips. "Before I came along, you thought magic was unreal, and look at us now. It's fine if you don't want to believe me, but I'm telling you, something is going on in this damn town again and I'm going to figure out what. My magic wouldn't be going haywire for no reason. It's all connected. I just know it."

"Your magic is doing what now?"

"Oh. Yeah. I kinda can't access my magic anymore. I mean, I can, but it's all over the place. It's like I don't have control of it or something."

"Babe, that is serious!" I said, my voice rising. How many things was this girl going to keep from me? Did I really make it that hard for her to trust me? The wolf growled in agreement, and I shook him off. *No one asked you, asshole.* "Why didn't you tell me before?"

She waved a hand over my body as if that answered everything.

"You should have told me."

"Probably," she agreed. "I'm telling you now."

I arched an eyebrow. "Anything else you want to share?"

Reluctantly, Billie dug into her back pocket and pulled out an old photograph. Her fingers trembled when she passed it my way, resting the ragged paper in the palm of my hand. I inspected the photo, my eyes gliding from Peyton to the girl beside her. *What the hell is this shit now?* Looking up from the photograph, I peered at Billie through hooded eyes. "What's this supposed to be?"

"Morgan. That's Morgan."

Around us, the air got so thick I choked on it. This wasn't possible. None of this was possible. For all I knew, the girl was one of Peyton's friends and Billie was grasping at straws. Still, something about the way Peyton looked at the redhead in the picture gave me pause. It wasn't a friend. Whoever this was, she meant so much more.

"Where did you find this?" I asked, my body hollow.

"The house Morgan lived in. It's abandoned now, but the photo was there. I told you I'm not making this crap up. Do you believe me now?"

My voice caught in my throat, and I swallowed thick saliva before speaking. "I want to. I really want to."

"But you don't."

"It's not that." I took a step toward her, and my heart shattered when she stepped back. Hurt pooled behind her eyes, and I hated that it was me who caused it. I did want to believe Billie, more than anything. Yet what she was saying made no sense to me. What kind of spell could erase a person from existence? From the memories of an entire town? Sure, weirder shit happened in Shadowhurst, especially in the last few months, but this was so far fetched, I couldn't wrap my mind around it.

Billie crossed her arms over her chest and sighed. "Then what do you think is going on then?"

I didn't fail to hear the frustration in her voice.

"What if it's your magic that's doing all this?"

"What?"

"Your magic. You said it's been wonky, right? Maybe it's making you see things that aren't really there. I've been looking into those black lines, and I haven't found much, but Sav said that two people need to be on the same page for a mate bond to click in. What if all of this is connected? It can't be a coincidence that you began having these memories right when your magic got weird, and the black lines went away."

Before me, Billie's face dropped, and she shook her head as though she was trying to shake my words off. As though they dirtied her somehow. "You've got to be kidding me," she ground out. "I literally just showed you a picture of our missing friend and that's what you're thinking about? The stupid mate bond? Something that might not even exist for us?!?"

I reached for her, but she held up her hand, motioning for me to stop.

"I need to get out of this place," Billie said, walking to the door.

"Okay, good. Where do you want to go?"

Casting me a side glance, she twisted the handle and opened the door to step out. Her hair whirled in the wind drifting in, and the darkness of the evening settled over her features. "I'm going back to the Crystal Cauldron. Alone."

"Babe, please! Let's not do this," I begged.

"It's fine," she said. "I'm not mad. I get where you're coming from, I really do. But Morgan and Lorelei are in danger, whether or not you want to believe it. Maybe we should take some time to ourselves tonight. I'll call you tomorrow."

"Who's Lorelei?"

Billie's gaze drifted to her feet, and she didn't bother looking at me when she stepped through the door. "Never mind," she whispered, disappearing from my sight.

Desperately, I wanted to chase after her. To drag her back to me and never let her leave my side, yet every step Billie took to disappear into the murkiness of the backyard glued me into place. I couldn't move and I couldn't pummel my way into her life right now. Not when she didn't want me in it.

Deep down, the wolf scratched at my skin and my head pounded with each one of his demanding pushes to get free.

This was a freaking disaster.

Feeling like the biggest piece of garbage to walk the earth, I gave Billie some time before walking out the front door. The night air greeted me with its icy fingers, and I breathed in the cold as I stomped to my car. The wolf growled again, and this time, I didn't force him away. Billie wanted time to herself, and I understood that. As much as I hated to admit it, she may have been right. There was so much turmoil in me, I didn't know what to do with myself, and I knew only one way to get rid of it, to make myself forget everything that happened, and I couldn't be near Billie when it happened.

The wolf growled as I backed the car out of the driveway and took off. No more holding back and no more trying to keep my shit together. I had to shift, and I had to do it now.

Chapter Sixteen

Billie

*R*iver literally made me want to punch a wall. Was he serious?!? The stupid black lines? That was what he thought about while I straight up shoved proof that Morgan existed into his stupid hands? Honestly, if I didn't love the guy, I would have probably knocked his teeth in. Lucky for him, one of us had the common sense to keep a cool head, and now that I was out of the house and on my way to the Crystal Cauldron, my head was cooler than ice.

Peddling as fast as my legs could manage, I rode my bike down Main Street, trying the entire time not to recount every second of my infuriating conversation with River. Trying and failing, of course.

It can't be a coincidence... No freaking kidding, hunter! None of this is a coincidence!

When I reached the Crystal Cauldron, I was so pissed that I sweat through my sweater. My hair clung in wet clumps to the rear of my neck, and I was breathing so fast, I wasn't even sure I was inhaling anymore. *This guy better switch his story soon or we're going to have a serious problem!*

Dumping the bike at the entrance, I looked around the empty street and pushed the door open. The overhead bell screamed to announce my arrival and I cringed from the sound. Shadows filled the shop, and when I slammed the door shut, the sign Ms. Broussard hung at closing scraped the glass with a loud screech.

Setting my shoulders, I approached the front counter.

"Ms. Broussard? It's Billie!"

A mop of white hair poked through the small door behind the counter. "Hi, dear," Ms. Broussard said, a welcoming smile spreading on her face. "A little late in the day for a visit, is it not?"

I swallowed hard, pressing my hands into the glass top to keep steady.

"Everything all right, Billie?"

"Not really," I whispered. "I'm sorry to bother you this late. I needed to get out of the house, and I didn't know where else to go."

"Sweetheart!" the shop owner exclaimed, gesturing for me to round the corner. "You are always welcome here! Come in, come in! I've just put on a fresh pot."

We walked in silence down the tight corridor leading to Ms. Broussard's apartment. Every step relaxed me, and I couldn't help but feel grateful for the mood-altering runes the woman had etched into the doorways of her home. Though the fight with River still lingered in the back of my mind, by the time we reached her living room, I no longer wanted to use him as a punching bag. *One small step at a time,* I thought and slumped into the sofa. My head dropped away while I waited for Ms. Broussard to bring her token tray of tea and cookies, and the pressure in my temples dissipated with every minute that passed.

By the time the shop owner returned, I was basically liquid.

Ms. Broussard handed me a cup of tea, and chamomile permeated the surrounding air. I inhaled the scent, sipping slowly and letting the heat of the drink warm my chest.

"Thank you," I said between gulps. "I needed that."

"Why don't you tell me what brings you here, dear?" Ms. Broussard said. Her gray eyes ran over me as she spoke, making me melt into the couch cushions. "Boy troubles, perhaps?"

I nodded in shame. "Yep. Sort of."

"Hmm..."

"River still doesn't believe me. Like at all. And to top it off, he thinks I'm doing this to myself. Why would I want to be crazy? I tried to tell him what Vic found in the Book of Darkness, and he didn't want to hear it. Why is he being this way?"

Swirling a silver spoon in her cup, Ms. Broussard pursed her lips into a tight line and scrunched her forehead. Her caramel skin fell into a million folds, and she tilted her head to the side as she thought of the next thing to say. None of it made me feel the least bit better.

"Men are interesting creatures," the shop owner breathed out. "Shifter males especially. I suspect you both have a temper not so easily calmed. Give him time, and yourself as well. Things will become clearer come morning."

"I doubt he'll all of a sudden believe me, morning or not. This isn't something sleep can fix. River thinks I'm making everything up and that *I'm* the reason my magic isn't working. Oh, and that those stupid lines are gone because of me! Can you imagine? That's what he's thinking about right now! Idiot."

"Mate bonds are important to shifters," Ms. Broussard said. "And he is a shifter, dear."

"That's not the point! I just need him to trust that I'm telling the truth. Why can't he do that?"

The shop owner looked over my shoulder to the small kitchenette behind us. Her eyes grew glassy and the wrinkles on her forehead smoothed out until they were completely gone. When her gaze found mine again, the woman looked ten years younger. Man, what I wouldn't give to look like that at her age.

Her lips twitched and the smallest hint of a smile spread over her face. "If someone told you magic isn't real, would you take their word for it? Or that the sky is red? The earth flat?"

Well, when you put it that way...

"It's not the same thing. Morgan is in danger. I need him to put his crap aside and help me deal with it."

"Perhaps he is," Ms. Broussard said. "Simply not in the same way you are."

Was River dealing with it? I had no idea. From what I could see, he was pretty dead set on convincing himself none of this was happening and it drove me wild. It was as if he was purposefully sticking his head in the sand. No matter how much River may not have wanted to believe it, people were freaking disappearing!

Still, what he said about my magic and the maybe-bond stung. For some reason, I couldn't get it out of my head. Was there a chance River was right? Could I be blocking those damn lines somehow and screwing with my own magic?

Shaking my head, I took another sip of tea and settled the cup on the small coffee table at my feet. "Even if he's right about the bond thing, that doesn't explain Morgan," I said. "Or Lorelei."

"Lorelei?" Ms. Broussard asked.

Right. Of course, she didn't remember her either. Of course.

"Lorelei is a mind reaper. One of the resistance leaders. She's gone too. And same as Morgan, no one remembers her but me. It's seriously messed up."

Next to me, Ms. Broussard lifted the corners of her mouth in a tired smile. She stood up, pretty quickly for someone her age, and beelined for a pile of books on the windowsill. Pushing a few tomes aside, the shop owner wrapped her scrawny fingers around a leather spine and swung back to the couch. As she neared, recognition flooded my system and my jaw dropped to my feet.

"Marcus' journal!" I yelped, glaring at the small notebook. "I completely forgot about it!"

"I've held onto it since..." Ms. Broussard weighed her words. "...Well, since you were taken. I had the distinct urge to read through it today and the name you mentioned, Lorelei, it sounds familiar."

Settling into the couch, the shop owner flipped the aged pages, inspecting each line as one would inspect a crime scene. Her eyes danced over Marcus' immaculate handwriting, fingers drifting over the ink while she read. When she neared the last few pages of the journal, she turned it around in her lap to face me. "Ah! There it is!" Ms. Broussard said excitedly. "Most of this is nonsense, as far as I can tell, but I knew I remembered that name for a reason."

She pointed to a particularly short sentence, and I read it aloud.

"'The graveyard is the answer, but Lorelei disagrees'."
My legs froze. "What graveyard? Answer to what?"

"That remains to be found out," the shop owner said.
"There was no other mention of it here, nor of this Lorelei."

"So we got nothing?"

"Not exactly."

I dared to look up at Ms. Broussard, and the twinkle in
her eyes made me buckle back. "What do you mean?"

"There is only one graveyard I could think of that may
hold a shadower's interest. Why, I am uncertain, though I
believe that is the place Marcus was speaking about when he
wrote this." The shop owner clutched my hand, pressing it
into the journal. "There is an old graveyard in Carriage Hill.
One that has not been used for many years. Most locals
refuse to set foot in it because of the dark history it holds."

"Dark history?"

Ms. Broussard's grasp on my hand deepened. "This was
the place they buried all those that died during the witch
burnings many years ago."

"A witch graveyard," I whispered.

Despite my earlier outburst, I reached for my cellphone
and opened my last text conversation with River, deleting
the strand of curses I started to write when I was still upset.
Choosing my words carefully, I typed the only thing that
came to mind.

*I don't want to argue. We have a lead. Graveyard in
Carriage Hill. Tomorrow after school. Want to come with?*

Making sure the message was sent, I pocketed the phone
and spun around to the journal. It wasn't much to go by, but
it was a good lead and I had to check it out. There was something in that graveyard that drew Marcus' attention, and it

was important enough for him to jot it down. I may not have known what drew Marcus to this place, but I knew well enough not to disregard it. Perhaps that graveyard was the answer after all. Perhaps it was the answer I needed to find my friends.

Chapter Seventeen

River

The sky welcomed a setting sun, bleeding hues of oranges and reds as I followed Billie to the graveyard in Carriage Hill. We marched in silence with her turning around every so often to make sure I was still following. She didn't have to keep checking. I would follow her to the end of the world.

"Is that it?" I asked, pointing to a set of wrought-iron gates in the distance.

Billie's gaze followed my extended index finger and her eyes lit up with excitement. Her hand reached for mine, and I took it without a second thought, keeping up pace as she took off toward the gates. When we approached, I inspected the entrance to the graveyard and frowned.

This place was definitely a piece of crap.

Ivy crawled over the rusty gates, covering every inch of the bars. Above, a plaque hung on for dear life from with illegible writing decorating its metal. I could vaguely make out the word 'graveyard' in the jumbled mess and breathed out heavily, relieved we were at least in the right place.

Beside me, Billie's nails dug into my flesh and her face twisted in disgust.

"Well, this is gross," she muttered under her breath. "At least we know no one else will be here."

Let's freaking hope so...

I nudged her forward, moving closer to the gates. The metal gave way comfortably when I pushed them open, tearing the overgrown grass with ease. Billie looked to me and shrugged as if to say 'what could go wrong' and bile crept up my throat.

A hell of a lot could go wrong if our past was any indication.

Refusing to let my doubts cloud my judgment, I reaffirmed my grip on her hand and we walked through together. Before us, a narrow, wild walkway unfolded, and we followed it into the unknown. It was quiet in the graveyard, too quiet for my liking, and I found myself scanning the sides as we walked. There was nothing out of the ordinary here. In fact, the place was exactly what one would imagine an abandoned cemetery to resemble. Except I knew better. This wasn't any cemetery. This was the place they buried the witches they burnt. Simply thinking of it made me nauseated. People did all this, my own damn people. This was where it all began, and I couldn't help but be disgusted with my kind for allowing this to happen.

Witch hunters are the fucking worst. I can't believe I actually wanted to be like these people.

"You okay?" Billie asked, nudging my side.

A tired smile played on my lips when I looked down at her. "I hate it here. Humans are awful."

"It was a long time ago."

That doesn't make it okay.

"Hey," she whispered, pulling me to a stop. "This isn't who you are. The witches buried here?" She waved over the landscape before us. "They lived in a different time. Their deaths are not on you."

"That's not really true," I said. "My ancestors did all of this. They burnt these women for no other reason than who they were. Took them away from their families and tossed them in here to be forgotten. It's not right."

"No, no, it's not. But it's not who you are, and that's what you should be concentrating on. You're not like your ancestors, River. I mean, you're a freaking shapeshifter, remember? The people who put these witches in the ground would have wanted you dead too. You're on the same side as every woman buried here." Billie looked around. "Why don't we get in there and see what we can find?"

Shaking my head, I let her pull me forward until we were so far from the gates, I could barely make them out behind us. A small hilltop stretched before us, and my teeth chattered as I looked at the protruding headstones. There were so many, I couldn't count them all. Each one stabbed my heart anew until I couldn't move. Beside me, Billie's eyes wetted, and though she tried to hide it, a single tear escaped and rolled down her cheek.

"Come on," I urged. "Looks like there's a clearing over there. Let's check it out."

We stomped past the headstones, careful not to disturb the wildflowers growing around each one. As we passed, I tried to read every name I could make out, committing them to memory and adding them to my own personal Hell. I would not forget these names for as long as I lived. They deserved to be remembered.

My head was pounding by the time we reached the clearing, and Billie froze in her spot.

"What the hell?" she hissed, dropping to the ground.

Her fingers traced over the dirt, picking up random items she found and bringing them up to her face to study further. When she picked up something that resembled a knife, I had to step in. This girl was going to need a tetanus shot when we were done here.

"Um, maybe don't touch everything," I suggested. "This stuff could be dangerous."

As though she was trying to taunt me, Billie raised a filthy rock to my face and waved it around. "It sure as shit is!" she exclaimed. "These are spell remnants. All of them. Someone did some serious magic here."

"Recently?" I asked, my eyes widening. I glanced around us, my heart rate speeding up as worry set in. Reaching into my jacket, I pulled out the gun Jayden let me borrow and kept it at my side.

Billie took one look at me and burst out laughing. "Calm down! There's no one here. This stuff hasn't been touched in ages."

I most definitely will NOT calm down. "So, what kind of spell was it?"

"I'm not sure." She shrugged, touching another weird-looking rock, and driving me crazy. "More than one, I'm guessing. See this here?" She pointed to a carving at the base of the rock in her hand. "That's an amplifier rune. Witches use this to give their spells more oomph if you know what I mean. That one there is to call on the fire element, and this one is for water. There's more of these all over, so I'm thinking witches came here to perform spells frequently. I wonder why *this* place though."

"Maybe they preferred to be close to their past?" I asked.

Billie arched an eyebrow. "Maybe."

Something about the way she said it made me think she didn't agree with me one bit. I could see the wheels turning in her brilliant head and it made me even more uneasy. This place was another puzzle for Billie, and I wondered if being here would do more harm than good. She was already unraveling and hanging out in a damn cemetery full of witch remains and weird spell remnants were likely not the best way to get her head on straight.

"I don't think we'll find anything here," I said. "We should probably head back before dark."

"Not yet."

As I watched Billie search the graveyard, my pulse beat a steady drum against my skin. She dragged me here, hoping to find a clue that cast some light on her delusions, and I could sense her disappointment as though it was my own. Of course, I knew this place would be a dead end. There was nothing to find because we weren't looking for anything real. I only wished Billie could finally understand that.

My eyes ran over her slender frame, and I watched her bend down next to one headstone. Brushing her palm across the slab, Billie's mouth gaped, and a gasp escaped her. I ran over, crouching next to her, and feeling my jaw unhinge. "Is that..."

"Graves," Billie answered, her eyes never leaving the name etched into the stone. "This is where she was buried."

Tears ran down her face and I reached around to hold her as she sobbed. Her body shook against mine, each tremble hurdling through me in furious beats. I had no words of comfort to give her. Mostly because I had no idea what she could have been feeling. If I found a grave that belonged to someone in my family, I'd probably pay my dues and move on. But this was different for Billie. She knew so little of her past that seeing this must have destroyed her. Nothing could be as final as a grave, and here we were, crouched at one that belonged to her long-lost family member.

I was about to say something—stupid no doubt—when my phone vibrated in my pocket shocking both of us. Eyes never leaving Billie, I picked it up and answered.

"River! Oh, thank God! Where are you?"

"Sav?" I asked, surprised to hear my best friend's voice on the other end. She sounded frantic and was loud enough for Billie to hear her through the phone. "What's wrong?"

"They're after me!" Savannah shrieked. "You need to get here now!"

Grabbing the phone from me, Billie pressed it to her ear, her face a pale sheet of fear. "Savannah? Where are you? Who's after you?"

"The High Coven," Savannah choked out. Her voice hiccupped and her breathing thundered on the line. "They're coming for me."

"Where are you right now?"

"My house. I'm alone, but I know they're outside."

Billie's shoulders shook and I could see her try to keep calm with no success. "Barricade all the doors and windows, do it now. Can you call Logan to come over?"

"Okay, yeah. I'll call him."

For Savannah to agree to accept help could only mean one thing. She was scared shitless.

"We're on our way," Billie said before hanging up. When she rose to stand, the conviction in her face made my nerves skyrocket. Wrapping her fingers around mine, she turned away from the tombstone and pulled me behind her. "How fast can you get us there?" she asked, not bothering to look back.

"Fast enough to get pulled over," I answered.

We ran down the walkway that led out of the graveyard and jumped in my car. I peeled out so quickly that dust rose from the ground as the tires squealed against the filthy pavement. Next to me, Billie's breath quickened as we drove back to Shadowhurst, speeding enough to get my license revoked if we got caught. I didn't care one bit. All I could think of while I drove was Savannah trapped in her house with the damn coven outside.

Please, let us get there in time.

Chapter Eighteen

Billie

I could sense the magic when we approached Savannah's farmhouse. Its sticky tendrils swirled in the air, calling to me in ways I had almost forgotten. Savannah wasn't exaggerating. The coven was definitely here.

Yet, I couldn't see them. At all.

"Something's wrong," I said to River as we crept along the large wraparound porch of Savannah's house. "I can't see any witches. But I can feel their magic."

"I can feel it too. Let's get inside and figure it out," River instructed.

I followed him to the front door, waiting impatiently while he texted Savannah to let us in. We were trying to stay as quiet as possible, though I knew there wasn't much point to it. If I could feel the coven, they could feel me as well. Plus, River wasn't exactly covert when he pulled into the driveway. Seriously, did no one pay attention to spy movies in this town? Kill the lights, park farther down the street, and ninja your ass to the destination. It wasn't that hard to follow.

Meanwhile, my boyfriend may as well have shot fireworks out of the sunroof when we arrived. I had to bite my tongue not to tell him off right there and then. Honestly, I was still annoyed as hell, but this wasn't the time to bite his head off. Savannah was in danger, and we had to get to her. Fast.

We waited a few excruciatingly long minutes when a loud scraping sound boomed on the other side of the wall and the door creaked open. Savannah's one eye peered through the small opening, and she looked us up and down before stepping aside.

"Finally," she said, annoyance in her voice. "Logan's keeping guard at the other door. I thought you guys weren't coming anymore."

"Of course we'd come," River said. "We were in Carriage Hill, not like we can fly here."

"Well, *they* sure did!" Savannah yelped and dragged the dresser she used to block the door back into place.

Following Savannah through her enormous house—mansion, really—I checked every window and came up empty. *Where are you assholes? And why are you even here?* My heart fluttered when we finally reached Logan, whose face was paler than usual. Even from here, I could tell he knew we had no shot against the coven if they decided to get inside. *Smart guy.*

"About time, mates," Logan said, earning himself a deep growl from River. "They haven't made a move yet. Think they're gone?"

I shook my head. "Nope. There's serious magic all around this place, I could feel it as soon as we parked. How did you know they were here?" I asked, turning to Savannah.

"I saw them," Savannah answered. "I was in the living room reading and I saw someone run by the window. When

I went to look, four witches were standing outside. They kept watching me. It was like the creepiest thing I've ever seen. I called you right away."

"They just watched you?" River asked.

Good question, babe.

"Uh-huh," Savannah said with a nod. "Like I said, creepiest shit ever."

Looking around, I struggled to wrap my head around what was going on. Why would the witches show up at Savannah's house to stand outside and do nothing? If they planned on attacking her, they would have done so already. And why attack her at all? Savannah was a human—a witch hunter, sure—but a human, nonetheless. There was no point for the coven to target her.

I didn't understand any of it.

"And you haven't seen them outside since you called us?" I asked.

"Nope. But you said they're still there, right? That you can feel them?"

Sighing, I turned back to the window. "Yep. Why would they—"

A bright flash burst to our right and River jumped in front of me, shielding me with his body. Even behind his wide shoulders, I could see shades of blue as the light intensified and grew in Savannah's living room. We huddled together, eyes wide open and lips trembling as we watched the blue light spread before us, pulsating as it expanded. Pushing past River, I took a few shaky steps forward to see clearer.

"What in the actual shit?" I cursed, breath hitching in my throat.

The blue light expanded further, forming a perfect ball

of energy that took up half the room. Focusing my eyes, I noticed the glow darken in the center as the ball grew outward. Inside, my magic vibrated, and though I was still terrified, feeling magic again was absolutely amazing. My legs tensed up and sweat dripped down my back while I watched the ball's center tighten up. The light in it grew dense until shapes formed within it, and by the time I understood what was happening, it was too late.

Figures emerged from the blue ball, filling Savannah's house with their sinister grins. One by one, the high priestesses stepped forward and my heart dropped to my knees.

A portal? What the hell, Sebyl?

That a portal had just opened up in Savannah's living room was beyond me and I worked to blink reality away in some pathetic attempt at pretending this wasn't actually happening. The coven had never been strong enough to open a portal before. Not for a lack of trying. Ever since I was a kid, I had watched as the high priestesses tried spell after spell to get one going with no luck. How did they do it now? And why open it here?

When I stopped gawking, ten head witches stood before us flanking the high priestesses on either side. My breath pummeled at my chest, and I tried not to let my emotions sway me when my gaze caught Sebyl's vicious stare. Her eyes betrayed no feeling. If I didn't know any better, I would have said this woman didn't know who I was. But she did know. For Goddess's sake, she helped raise me.

I wasn't sure what hurt more, the way Sebyl looked at me with such emptiness or that the other high priestesses didn't regard me at all. Rhiamon and Luna held their attention on Logan and River, while Theodora's blue eyes penetrated Savannah as if she was about to eat her alive.

Except for Luna's annoying bells chiming while she swayed, the room was silent.

No one moved and no one dared to speak. Except yours truly, of course.

My hands fisted and I widened my stance to face Sebyl. "What kind of magic is this?"

Sebyl cast a narrow glance at Theodora, then threw her head back and laughed. The tool actually freaking laughed. A fire burned in my belly, and I fought the urge to jump at her. The only thing keeping me in place was River's hand wrapped around my arm. I tried to shake him off, but he stayed strong, pulling me back toward our friends.

By the time Sebyl stopped her incessant cackling, I could tell everyone was as over these bitches as I was.

"How did you get a portal going?" I asked again.

"That is coven business," Sebyl said; a wolf's grin slapped on her face. "And you are no longer in the coven."

I moved closer, but Sebyl held a hand up, wiggling a wrinkled finger in my face. "I wouldn't do that if I were you," she warned. "You never know who might get caught in the crossfire."

My eyes jumped from her to the other priestesses, seeing magic dance on their fingertips. Theodora held her palm out, pointing to Savannah's chest, while next to her, Rhiamon and Luna directed their magic at River and Logan. My mouth dried and my jaw ticked watching them threaten my friends with their pathetic power.

Could I take them before they make a move?

I looked at the remaining head witches, noticing their arms stretch out toward our group. Probably not. *DAMN IT!*

Frustrated, I took a step back.

"Good girl," Theodora hissed, and I shot daggers her way with my eyes.

"What do you want from me?" Savannah choked out from behind Logan's protective stance. "You're seriously messing up the Feng Shui of my house."

Despite her attempt to sound confident, I could hear fear roll off every word. In my peripheral vision, I noticed Sebyl's lips twitch. She saw through Savannah's bullshit too. The high priestess took a few steps toward us, pausing several feet from me. Her dark bangs swayed across her forehead, and she narrowed her eyes past me at Savannah. "Time to begin," she said calmly to the other witches.

Sebyl linked her hands with Theodora and the head witch to her right. Her lashes fluttered and her nose seemed to elongate as the stupid grin on her face widened. In my chest, my heart thundered.

Not thinking, I threw my arms out and pushed every bit of magic out. My fingers spread wide, and I choked on air as I fought to summon the shadows within me. I was so close, so damn close. But not close enough. Before I could connect to my magic—something I wasn't even sure I could do—a fireball snuck into my view and my eyes bulged watching it. It cut across the room, flying toward me at an unbearable speed and rushing straight for my chest.

"Billie, NO!" River screamed, diving for me and knocking me to the ground.

My side hit the floorboards and my shoulder cracked from the impact. Above me, River rolled off, breathing heavily at my back. Scrambling to stand, I slid across the floor until I was on my knees. Vision blurring, I looked past the priestesses to the witch who threw the fireball and fury unfolded inside me. *She's going DOWN!*

Jumping up, I ran for her when a heavy gust of wind pushed me back. My legs kicked out from under me, heels dragging the floor as the wind carried me back. My back collided with the wall and my head shot from side to side, seeing the rest of my friends receive the same treatment. Our bodies glued down, we were trapped by winds so strong, I feared they would tear the house down. Twisting my arm, I fought against the current, shaking as I reached for the amethyst pendant on my neck.

I can play this game too.

My fingers tightened around the crystal, and I pulled for its energy, forcing my magic to find the element inside. Closing my eyes, I battled against my own incompetence, praying I had enough power to set us all free.

I didn't even have a second to try.

Before I could get a grasp on the pendant's energy, it shot out of my hand and landed at Sebyl's feet. The high priestess sneered. "Leave it alone, Wilhemina. Just because we're not allowed to hurt you, doesn't mean we will not try."

The hell?

"What are—"

The light of the portal exploded all around us. It rushed for Savannah in a brilliant swirl of blue magic with a force so fast, I had no time to blink before it hit her square in the chest.

She screamed. I screamed. We all freaking screamed.

Those were the last sounds I remember before the magic that held me in place pulled away and I dropped to the floor with a thud.

Chapter Nineteen

Billie

The witches inched closer while Savannah continued to scream, the blue light ripping at her flesh. Her body shook, hovering mid-air as she kicked and wailed against the magic. I must have been in shock because I could've sworn I saw her body flicker like a candle flame. Gathering myself off the floor, I crawled toward her, but Logan and River reached Savannah first. Their hands grabbed an ankle each and they pulled to get her down. I saw the struggle in their faces and the sweat roll down their foreheads.

Savannah's floating body would not budge.

Still shaking, I looked around the room, calculating our chances. Ten head witches and four high priestesses. This didn't look good. Even if we could free Savannah from whatever spell the coven had triggered, there was no way we were getting out of this alive.

My eyes darted from the witches to Savannah.

Not thinking, I bolted to my feet and flung myself toward her. Someone screamed my name, probably River, but it was too late. I was already flying at my friend and straight into that damn blue light that was doing Goddess knows what to her. My body twisted in the air, chest facing the rays that stretched from the portal.

"WILHEMINA!" Sebyl shrieked just as I barreled into the light.

The rays penetrated through me, locking me in place. Behind me, I heard Savannah's body fall to the floor. My skin tingled and my arms and legs locked in place. Around me, strange magic swelled, and I could feel it rush through me in waves. Pain unlike any I've felt before pierced my heart and my lungs struggled to gulp air. My hair clung to my face in wet patches, leaving my vision obscure. Not that I wanted to see what happened next.

I was definitely dead. For sure.

Deep inside, something stirred, and my eyes snapped open. Gaze downward, I saw the blue rays pushing into my chest, but something else was fighting against them.

My shadows!

Tears pricked at my eyes as I watched my magic come alive. Shadows spun over me, swirling their beautiful darkness over every inch of my body. The ground beneath the house shook and floorboards cracked as the earth under us rumbled. My arms splayed to the sides and my fingers spread wide as energy coursed through me and out into the world. Near to me, the head witches looked around, flustered, and unable to discern what was happening.

Better run, bitches.

The witches had no time to move when magic exploded from me, and heavy winds grasped them by the arms and legs and pulled them up. Their heads hit the ceiling and I cringed at the sound their necks made when they cracked.

The wind held them up for moments longer before I dropped my arms, causing the witches to crash to the floor. Surprisingly, some survived and were crawling away on all fours.

"Billie, watch out!" River shouted.

My attention turned to follow his eyes to the fireball Sebyl chucked at my face. With little control over my body, I gulped spit and watched the shadows rip my arm from my side and tug it outward. Water burst from my fingertips, meeting Sebyl's fireball head-on and extinguishing it in seconds.

The high priestess growled, and in her eyes, I saw panic and confusion rise.

Witches piled into the closing portal and a smile spread on my face as I watched them retreat. Rhiamon and Luna followed suit, leaving only Sebyl and Theodora standing in the living room. The blue light that threatened to kill Savannah—or do whatever the hell it was trying to do— pulled inward until all that was left between us were my shadows and the anger I held. My feet hit the floor and my chest rose and fell with each heavy breath.

Before me, Theodora grabbed Sebyl's arm to pull her into the portal only moments before it closed, and the room went dark.

Strong arms wrapped around me, and River pulled me into his chest. He stroked the top of my head, flooding me with desperate kisses while inspecting my body to make sure I wasn't hurt. I wasn't. At freaking all. How was that possible?

"What were you thinking doing that?" River scolded. "You could have died!"

"I know."

"That was the dumbest thing you ever did!"

"I know."

"We have no idea what that thing was, and you just threw yourself in there! Don't EVER do that again!"

"I know."

Footsteps shuffled behind us, and I struggled to loosen River's grip on me to turn around. When I looked up, Savannah was standing over me with Logan at her back. Her face was still pale, but I could see the color return with every breath she took.

The hunter trained her hazel eyes on me and licked her bottom lip. "Thank you. You saved me."

"Don't thank her!" River snapped. "That was a dumb move."

"Mate," Logan piped in, "she saved your best friend. Don't be an ass."

Every vein in River's neck popped and I had a distinct feeling that if I didn't stop this soon, someone was going to die. Probably Logan. Pressing my palm to his heart, I pushed on his chest until I had his full attention. "Babe, I'm fine. But Savannah almost died from whatever that thing was. Let's just be grateful that we all lived today. Okay?"

The look River gave me told me that this was definitely not okay. *Too bad, buddy. You're going to have to deal with it.* This was a win.

"Hey, so maybe a stupid question," Savannah said, "but how come that thing didn't hurt you? When I got blasted with it, it seriously felt like my skin was melting off my bones. My head was complete mush and I swear, I forgot my own damn name for a second."

"I don't know. I didn't feel any of that. It was weird

magic for sure, but not something like what you're describing," I said. "Wait, did you say you forgot your name?"

"Almost," Savannah said defensively, "I said *almost*."

"You guys don't think that's the spell?" I asked.

Savannah looked from me to River. "What spell?"

"Billie thinks there's a spell that's making us forget people."

"This again?"

Watching the two of them talk about me as though I wasn't in the room made the hair on my neck stand straight. My jaw clenched so tight, I could feel my teeth rattle together as I tried to breathe through the rage. Instinctively, I reached for my magic but was met with another wall. *Great, back to this crap.* Pulling out of River's embrace, I crossed my arms and cocked a hip to make sure they knew I wasn't having any of this.

"Yes, this again," I bit out. "There is a spell and tonight proved it. I knew the High Coven was behind this and whatever the hell that portal almost did to you, there's a very good chance it did it to our friends. I saw the same blue light right before Lorelei disappeared and I'm willing to bet the same thing happened to Morgan. The coven is using these portals to grab people and erase them. I have no clue why, but I'm going to find out. You two want to stand here and pretend it's not happening, fine! Don't get in my way!"

I was about to storm out when another hand grabbed my shoulder and twirled me around.

"I believe you," Logan said, his lavender eyes piercing into me.

Astonishment tore through me, and my eyebrows raised, gaze running over the mind reaper to see if he was messing with me. "You do?"

Logan nodded.

"Not you too," River sighed while Savannah rolled her eyes next to him.

I paid no attention to my stubborn shifter. "How come you believe me all of a sudden?"

"Not all of a sudden," Logan said. "Unlike these two, I never thought you were a nutter. And you might be on to something here with this portal business."

"You're serious? You're not just saying this to make me feel better cause I just almost died to save Savannah?"

Logan chuckled, peering at me through hooded eyes. "I'll do you one better," he said with a smirk. "I don't just believe you, Billie. I remember them too."

Chapter Twenty

Billie

I remember them too. Logan's words replayed in my head over and over until they were all I could hear. *What the heck, dude? You wait until now to tell me?!?* Everything about this situation was messed up, which is exactly what I told Logan right before I made River drive me home. As badly as I wanted to beat the reaper to a pulp for keeping this world-changing revelation from me, I couldn't deal with another fight. And a fight was exactly what I would get if I stuck around for longer. I could already see Savannah's eyes bulge out of her head when Logan told us he remembered Morgan and Lorelei. Whatever she was going to say next would not be pretty.

So, I left.

No, I didn't just leave. I bolted out of there like I was running cross-country for a damn gold medal.

Was it my finest moment? Probably not. Did I make it any better by keeping my mouth shut and avoiding River's concerned look the entire way home? Also, no. Yet, when I finally said good bye to my very confused boyfriend and climbed into bed, I could already feel the irritation subside. I won't lie, picturing Savannah tear into Logan after we left for keeping this shit from the group helped.

Teaches him right, the bastard.

I tossed and turned the entire night, wondering why it was just the two of us not affected by the spell the High Coven cast. And when I wasn't thinking about that, I was tearing my brain apart to figure out why the hell the coven needed to erase our friends in the first place. Oh, and of course, where in Goddess' name that portal came from and why its filthy magic didn't have the slightest effect on me.

In a nutshell, I was a sleepless mess by the time I had to get up and go to school.

Spending the rest of the day with my head in a book and my eyes trained on boring notes scribbled on blackboards, I made a pretty decent job of staying out of sight. I even managed to deflect the million questions Peyton had about last night and came up with excuse after excuse for why I couldn't hang out with everyone at lunch. By the time the last bell rang out, I hauled my shell of a person home and have been sitting out on the front porch ever since. My eyes watched nothing in particular and my head felt like an empty seashell, the wind rushing through from ear to ear. Honestly, I probably looked like a mental case, but hey, if the shoe fit...

The front door slid open, and I vaguely glanced in its direction.

"I'm running out to pick up a few things for dinner," Imala announced, sauntering past me. "Do you want to come with?"

Shaking my head, I resumed my obnoxious glaring at the driveway. "I'm good. Thanks, though." Feeling like the biggest pile of crap, I forced myself to look at her. "Thomas has you stocking up for his latest masterpiece, huh?"

"As always," Imala said with a frown. "One of these days, I'm going to come back with takeout just to see the look on his face."

A sad laugh was all I could manage. It was pathetic.

"You sure you're all right, Billie? I can tell him to pick up his own damn carrots and stick around?"

Imala's questioning eyes ran over me and I shrank in the chair. I loved spending time with her, but right now, I didn't want the company. It wasn't as though I could tell her what was really going on, so what good would it do? Best I stayed away from people for a while. At least until I could talk myself out of vanquishing Logan's sorry ass for lying this entire time. *Seriously, what a tool.*

Curling my lips, I looked up at Imala. "All good here," I lied. "Stressful day at school, but nothing an awesome dinner won't fix."

"Well, don't tell Thomas that," Imala teased. "His head is already so big, I don't see how he makes it through the front door."

Chuckling, she flipped her long hair over her shoulder and meandered to her car. Her high heels clicked on the pavement, swaying her hips from side to side as she departed. Tossing her Birkin on the passenger side, she was about to settle in when another car veered into the driveway. My eyes narrowed and I sighed loudly as River's Porsche pulled in and he popped his head out of the window.

"River, darling!" Imala exclaimed, peering at him over her sunglasses. "Come keep our girl some company while I run out. She had a bad day at school."

River smiled and climbed the steps to sit in the chair

opposite me. "Will do!" He raised his hand in a salute. "Keeping her company is my number one job."

We watched Imala pull out. As soon as her car was gone, I was met with a pair of sparkling emeralds tearing into me.

"So," River said, one eyebrow raised, "bad day at school?"

I growled and shook my head. "Bad day in life at this point, I think."

"Assuming you're not talking about the algebra test we have next week?"

"You got me!" I joked. "I don't know what could more stressful than a test! Oh, wait, how about the fact that our friends are freaking missing, and our other friend lied to everyone? No, you're right, it's the test."

River's brow furrowed and he leaned in, resting his elbows on his knees. *Serious? Not even a fake laugh? Ugh, boys. What good are they?*

"Yeah, about that..."

I looked at him wearily, trying to discern what bomb was about to drop in my lap. When River still didn't speak, my stomach dropped, and my knees trembled. Why was it that every time I thought my damn head was going to explode, everyone around me decided to make things worse? River hadn't even said anything yet, and I already knew that whatever fell out of his annoyingly full lips would not make me feel any better. Kicking me while I'm down was simply the Shadowhurst way.

Cracking my knuckles, I leaned into the chair and mentally put on my big girl pants. "Spit it out."

"Okay, don't freak out," he said, in that way that definitely made me freak the hell out. "I'm thinking maybe we don't jump to any conclusions with what Logan told us."

"Jump to conclusions? What conclusions could we jump to here? *I* remember our friends, *he* remembers our friends, the rest of you don't. The High Coven is up to some shit, and now, they have portals. I think that pretty much covers it."

"Right. But the thing is, and I have no clue how to say this without sounding like an ass." He paused to hold my gaze. "I don't trust Logan. Not even a little. Something is off about that guy, and for all we know, he's toying with us."

My jaw unhinged. "Do you really not believe me so badly that you're willing to call him a liar to prove it? Logan is telling the truth. I know he is."

"So why keep it from us this whole time?"

"That," I grumbled, "I don't know. But for some reason, neither I nor he are affected by this stupid spell the coven cast, and that's what we need to figure out."

"Have you talked to Vic or Peyton about this?"

"Not yet. I will, though. Vic's dropping by later, so I'll fill her in then."

The air grew warmer around us, and when I looked at River, I could see his eyes brighten a few shades. The shifter in him was not happy that I was back to my antics, but there was nothing I could do about it at this point. River and his wolf had to either get on board with what I had been trying to prove from the beginning, or they both had to get out of my way. I had no time to entertain their worries, and I certainly had no patience for it.

After a few dreadful minutes of complete silence, he finally relaxed his shoulders. "So, what can I do? I want to help you figure this stuff out."

The world's tiniest butterfly fluttered its wings in my stomach, and I smiled. "Can you talk to Logan? See why he kept all this to himself for so long? I think if I even *try* to speak to him right now, I might punch his teeth in."

"Sure thing." River chuckled and intertwined our fingers. "What are you going to do?"

Freak out. Try to breathe. Stress until my hair falls out.

"I have an idea and it might be a little crazy," I said. "I think I know how I can fix at least one of the things going wrong. Could be a dead end, but worth a shot."

His fingers tightened on mine until all the blood rushed from my hand. I held his grip, gritting my teeth, and yet, refusing to pull away. What I was about to tell River would likely not go over well, and if he needed to break my damn fingers to keep his shit together, I was going to let him.

Returning his firm grip, I tilted my head and took a deep breath. "I'm going back to the cavern. I have to fix my magic and I have to do it soon. If I don't, we could lose this fight before we even know what hit us."

Chapter
Twenty-one

River

"Yeah, that's not happening. No way."

"Excuse me?" Billie's face tensed and I could see her need to fight me rise to the surface. She had already made her mind up, but that didn't mean I had to agree with it. Returning to the cavern was a dumb idea, and I was going to make sure she knew that.

My fingers curled tighter around hers, and I had to bite my tongue to keep from squeezing. "Why would you even want to go back there?" I asked. "That place put you through Hell, and now, what? You want to ask for more?"

Billie pulled away from me and I instantly missed her touch.

"I need my magic," she announced, leaving me no room to argue. "This isn't up for debate. I'm going, and I'm going alone."

"That's a hard no."

"Wasn't asking for permission here," she snapped.

Clenching my jaw, I dared to meet her eyes. "Babe, if

you think I'm letting you go back to that damn place on your own, you're crazy."

The look on her face told me my choice of words was far from great. I probably should have reconsidered using that term around her. Seeing that Billie had spent the last while trying to convince all of us she wasn't insane, my outburst was a trigger if I've ever heard one. I immediately regretted saying it.

And the prick of the year award goes to... "You know what I mean," I said, hoping it would lighten the mood. It did not. "Let me come with you, in case something happens."

Billie looked as though she was thinking it over, and a glimpse of hope fluttered its wings in my chest. I should have known better by now, she wasn't debating letting me tag along, she was only looking for the words to let me down easy. Leave it to Billie to worry about my feelings when she was about to throw herself into danger. *Stubborn, impossible woman!*

"Look," she finally uttered, "it's not that I don't want you there. I really do. But if you come with me, all I'll be thinking about is your safety, and that will just get in the way. I need to do this alone so I can concentrate on my magic and not be distracted. Besides, we need you here to stay close to Savannah. The coven wanted her for some reason, and I know Sebyl. Once she has her sights on something, she's not letting go. A dog with a bone, that one."

I could not begin to describe how much I despised the logic in her thinking.

"And you said you'll talk to Logan, remember? See why he's been hiding remembering Morgan and Lorelei."

Fucking Logan. The last thing I wanted was to talk to that pretentious tool, but Billie was right. If he truly did remember these people, we needed to know how and why. My mind raced and my legs tensed when I pictured the upcoming conversation. A part of me wanted him to be lying, to come out and say the whole thing was a cry for attention or something else equally stupid. A bigger part of me knew that wasn't the case. Guilt pulled at my heart when I thought about all the time I wasted trying to make Billie see reason when I was the one who couldn't see what was right in front of him.

I was wrong not to believe her.

People were in danger—people that were apparently our friends—and instead of helping her understand it, I pushed the idea away and pretended it wasn't happening. No matter how deranged the entire thing sounded, Logan's revelation put everything in a perspective.

Billie wasn't going mental. The rest of us were.

Just freaking wonderful.

In front of me, Billie's face lit up in a genuine smile and I twisted to see what made her happy for the first time in what seemed like forever. When Victoria's heart-shaped face popped into view, my heart sank. I wanted more time alone with Billie, especially now that I knew what a bastard I've been. Instead, I had to share her with other people. That wasn't even the worst of it. The absolute worst part was that every time someone else showed up, it was never good news. Victoria especially. I wondered what damn catastrophe she was going to drop in our laps this time. I couldn't handle it. My wolf couldn't either.

Worse, I wasn't sure Billie could.

"Vic!" Billie yelped and jumped up to greet her friend. Her silky hair pooled around her shoulders, and I battled the urge not to touch it as she strolled past me. "I have some great news! Logan remembers too! I was flipping right about the whole thing!"

Victoria smiled and cocked her hip to the side, peering over Billie's shoulder to shoot a smile my way. I didn't return it.

"That's awesome!" she exclaimed. "Wait, why didn't he say anything before?"

"No clue. River is going to find out, but this is good, right? It means it's all actually happening. I mean, that's not good. You know what I'm saying."

The girls chuckled as though they exchanged an inside joke I wasn't privy to, and I crossed my arms, frowning. "Did she tell you what happened with Savannah?"

The two grew silent and it took a few moments for Billie to start speaking. I watched her recount last night's events with such ease, it felt almost unreal. Like it was a movie she watched and not a personal hell we'd all stepped into. My eyes burned with every filthy detail drudged up again and by the end of Billie's story, I felt as though I was right back in Savannah's house watching the coven reap havoc on all of us.

When Billie stopped talking, Victoria rubbed her chin and narrowed her eyes. "A portal, huh? That's messed up."

"I know." Billie sighed and fumbled with the zipper of her jacket's sleeve. "Have you seen them try one since I've left? In all my years with the coven, I have known no one to succeed in creating a portal. How the hell did they manage it now?"

"News to me. From what I know, the high priestesses gave up on portal magic a while back. Something about not being able to work the moon in their favor. If they got one going, it took some serious mojo and I have no idea where they could have pulled that much power from."

Something about what Victoria said made Billie freeze. She dropped her hands to her side and chewed her bottom lip so intensely, I thought she might draw blood. Blood rushed from her face, and when her gaze found Victoria's, there was darkness hiding in her eyes. "Say that again," Billie demanded.

"Say what again?"

"The moon. You said something about working the moon."

Victoria arched an eyebrow and stole a glimpse my way. "To open a portal, a witch needs more magic than she can summon from the elements. The only way to do it is to use moon magic to amplify the spell, but it has to work in perfect symbiosis with elemental magic. Portals haven't been used for centuries, not since the fae disappeared and took their powers with them. That's why the high priestesses abandoned the entire thing. Even when they were attempting to use the blood moon, it still didn't give them enough kick."

"Blood moon?" I asked. My brain hurt just listening to these two talk. It felt similar to missing a school lecture and then being called up to recite the whole thing in front of the class. I hated not knowing things, and I hated being the only one that didn't follow the conversation. It was brutal.

Turning on her heels, Billie took a few steps to stand near me and the annoyance that boiled in my veins cooled down. She placed a hand on my hair, relaxing every tense muscle.

"It's a solar eclipse of sorts," she explained. "Happens twice a year, more or less, and is one of the strongest nights of the year to work moon magic. Maybe..." Her words trailed off and she looked into the distance. Billie's eyes glazed over, and she tilted her head to the side. "Vic, can the blood moon amplify the elemental magic in a person?"

"You don't think?" Victoria asked, leaving me in the dark again.

I cleared my throat. "Can you two stop talking in riddles and let the non-witch in on what you're thinking?"

"Every person is born under a different elemental sign," Billie said. "You know them as zodiac signs, but to a witch, they are so much more. Each sign correlates to a distinct element. Fire, water, air, and earth. In humans, the elemental energy is tiny, almost inconceivable. Not surprising since they don't have active magic in their blood as we do. One good thing we inherited from the fae. Witches use elemental energy to fuel their magic. Crystals, herbs, natural objects, whatever."

"So, what does the blood moon have to do with it?"

Billie's lips turned upward, and next to her, Victoria breathed out a laugh.

"We use moon cycles to strengthen our hold on elemental energy, give our magic a boost of sorts, and connect us to our fae creators. The blood moon is pretty much the best time to work powerful spells, which would explain why the coven would use it to attempt creating a portal. A portal is tough as shit to pull off, so they would need all the help they could get. Think of the blood moon as a battery. Combine it with the elements and whatever spell you're casting, and BOOM!"

"...Okay," I choked out. "But you just said the coven could never get the spell to work before."

"They couldn't," she agreed. "But I think I know how they did it this time."

Close to us, Victoria's eyes widened to saucers. "You think they're getting energy from people, not items."

"Yep," Billie said with a nod. "Not just any people. People born under the blood moon. Their elemental energy would be stronger than any item out there, even if they were human. Being born under a blood moon is a big deal. That shit burrows deep and stays there."

"That can't be right," Victoria whispered. "Witches don't drain energy from living creatures. It's against the code."

I scoffed. "You think the coven cares about a code? Those bitches are evil."

"We need Morgan, Lorelei, and Savannah's birth dates. Test them against previous blood moon cycles to see if I'm right. And we need to figure out if this is something that can even be done. I'm pulling at strings here." Shoulders tensed, Billie nipped at her lip again while calculating something else in her head. "If this is what they're up to, we still have some time."

"How do you figure?"

"They got Morgan and Lorelei, but we stopped them from taking Savannah. That means they only have two of the elements so far. They'd need all four, plus the spirit element to bind the circle."

"But that's you," I whispered, terror gripping my bones. "You have spirit blood, we already know that."

Billie blew a strand off her face and squeezed my shoulder. "I wasn't born under a blood moon, so I'm safe. But someone else out there isn't as lucky. Someone that—"

"Was a spirit fae descendant like you," Victoria choked out. "Great, back to this again."

I couldn't agree with her more. Billie's past, and the whole Graves business, was a serious cock-block when it came to figuring things out. Somehow, the road always led back to her family history with the fae, and we knew literally nothing about it. If Billie was right, finding another person with the spirit element in their blood would be next to impossible. The only thing that gave me hope was that the High Coven would be just as stuck as we were.

"Okay, so we need to find out why the coven targeted these girls and who they're going after next. And find the exact spell they're using," I said.

"And you need to see what Logan knows," Billie added.

Standing before us, Victoria stayed quiet, and it made me weary. Her fingers played with the inky strands of her ponytail and her gaze glared directly through us as though she wasn't aware we were next to her at all. The witch's eyebrows curled and uncurled, and her chest moved up and down as she drifted off in thought.

"Vic?" Billie asked, concern soaking her every word. "You okay?"

Victoria shook her head and grinned. "I might know someone who can help. You two find out the dates of the girls that vanished, and Savannah, and I'll figure out the spell thing. I'll come back soon, hopefully with answers."

Before we could press her for information, the witch twirled around and bolted down the driveway, leaving us in the dust.

Chapter Twenty-two

Billie

*B*lood pumping, I trudged into the dark belly of the cavern. Each step taking me further in sent terror up my legs and I had to fight the urge to turn around with every passing second. Luckily, River finally agreed to let me do this alone, though he was definitely not happy about it. No, that's not correct. He was downright pissed. Either way, he let me be and followed my instructions to talk to Logan. With Vic going to wherever the hell she ran off to, splitting up was our best bet. Cover all ground to save time and whatever. Still, now that I was back in the stupid cavern with my heart trapped in my throat, I was regretting not letting him tag along.

Too late now, loser. Keep your ass moving and get a grip.

Setting my shoulders, I faced the tunnel ahead and walked through, dragging my heels across the rock. My head was a jumbled mess. Torn between memories of this heinous place and hopes of getting my magic back. If I was right and the coven was using elemental energy from actual freaking people to create portals, I was going to need my magic to stop them. Granted, I wasn't even sure that was the case, or if coming here would even help.

I had to try though, right? Right. Definitely.

Rounding another tight corner, I gasped when I looked up. Narrowing my eyes to see in the dark, my pulsed raced as visions of this place came flooding back. I remembered being dragged by chains and every pain I felt then rushed through me. My hand reached for a wrist, rubbing the spot where the shackles held me prisoner for so many days on end. Except for this time, I was free and no one forced me to my knees and beat me senseless. This was my choice, and I had to keep going.

"Not today, Satan," I hissed into the air and sped up.

It didn't take long to reach the place where we defeated Daria and her shifters. The air was wet and cold, and as I looked toward the drop into nothingness ahead of me, shivers crawled over my body. My eyes dodged past the large boulders I tore from the cavern walls and my hands shook, remembering the strength I felt when I connected to the elemental energy inside me.

I shut my eyes, letting the memories of that day swamp my senses.

My lids fluttered as I replayed every step I took to gain more power. I reached for the shadows sitting dormant in my blood. Deep down, I could feel them tremble, but they were too far to call on.

"Shit!" I shrieked, snapping my eyes open. *Why wasn't this working?*

Resolve flooded me and I closed my eyes again, trying one more time. When nothing happened, I sighed and leaned against the wall, slumping my head in defeat.

This was a stupid idea.

Running my fingers through my hair, I pulled it back and let frustration overtake me. I was so sure this would work, I didn't even let myself consider the alternative. That my magic was gone for good and I was as useless as one could get.

"We meet again," a familiar, song-like voice called from the darkness.

I jumped, hitting my shoulder on the wall and wincing as the pain rolled down my arm. Close to me, dense shadows swirled in the murky air, and I didn't have to try hard to make out the man standing amidst them. His body swayed from side to side like a pendulum, and though the darkness concealed his features, I could sense his traitorous grin all the same.

The shadow man floated closer, stopping a few feet away from me. "Welcome back, daughter. I was wondering how long it would be until you returned."

"Ugh, you again," I hissed. "Came to see my utter failure, I take it?"

A rumble sounded in the shadow man's chest, and it took me a second to realize he was laughing. *Bastard.*

"On the contrary," he purred. "Coming here was a sensible move. Fruitless, though sensible."

Awesome, more riddles. "What happened to my magic?" I demanded, burying my weight into the ground. "What did this place do to me?"

"The question is not 'what', daughter."

"Huh?"

"Also not the question."

Jaw ticking, I shoved my hands in my pockets and kicked a nearby rock in his direction. "Enough with the games.

What's the question you think I should be asking since you're so damn brilliant?"

"Why," he sang.

"Why what, weirdo?"

The shadow man sneered, and I swear I saw red. This guy was so infuriating, I could seriously see myself strangle the life right out of him. If I could touch him, that is. Or if I could even kill him. Whatever the heck he was. Flashes of this stranger professing to be my father burst before me, and I nearly laughed out loud at the thought. *Some dad, huh? No, thank you.*

I wanted to get out of this place and back to the real world, but before I could make a move, the shadow man spoke again.

"*Why* is your magic trapped?" he asked. "That is the correct question."

I scoffed. "Okay, so why? Why is it gone?"

"Not gone, daughter. Trapped."

"Goddess, what are you talking about? What's the difference? It's not freaking there. Gone, trapped, who cares? I want to know how to get it back!"

A shadow burst from his fuzzy form and the rock I kicked rolled back toward me, landing at my feet. "Stones are an interesting thing," the man said. "So very unassuming and yet, so powerful at the same time."

"What are you going on about now?" I asked. Then my mind cleared. I found the small staurolite in my pocket, holding it up between us. "You left this for me, didn't you?"

Shadows swirled as the man nodded slowly.

"Why is this stone important?"

"You see, my dear," he sang, "the 'why' is always key."

A frustrated grunt left my lips, and I tightened my grip

on the staurolite, trying to decipher his vague sentiments. "Does this thing have something to do with my magic being gone? Trapped. Whatever."

Another slow nod.

Awesome progress. Can I buy a vowel next?

"How do I use it to fix myself?"

"You are not broken," the shadow man said. "You are simply not yet ready for what you are to become. Keep the stone by your side, and when it is time, I will return that which is missing."

My head pounded and my fingers tightened into fists at my side. "YOU did this? Did you take my magic from me? Bastard!"

I lunged for him, throwing myself into the abyss of his body. The shadow man shifted to the side, twisting out of the way and making me stumble like a damn fool to my knees. Rock hit bone and I cringed from the pain, refusing to cry out. This asshole would not see any weakness from me, not now and not ever. *Cocky prick!*

Scrambling on the ground, I turned and looked toward him. "I don't understand your game here."

"All will be clear soon, daughter. When you are ready, your magic will return. It will be complete, as shall you."

Complete? *What does that even MEAN?!?* My mind unraveled as I tried to make sense of his stupid words. I was already complete before. I had magic. I had my shadows. More than that, the last time I was in this forsaken place, I had elemental powers I never dreamed of. I could control the earth, the water, the air—

Oh, my freaking, Goddess.

"The fire element," I breathed out. "It was the only one I

was missing. The only element I couldn't tap into when I was here. That's what you mean, isn't it?"

His shadows spread across the cavern, reforming into a man's shape on my right. My head turned to face him, and in seconds, he vanished, only to reappear on my left. The entire thing felt like a game of cat and mouse, except I was both the cat and the mouse in this equation. And he, well, he was something else altogether.

The darkness surrounding him flickered and his already sheer form shimmered. Instinctively, I reached out to stop him from leaving, knowing full well that it wouldn't do any good. Before he disappeared, the man turned to look down at me, pointing a finger at my chest.

"Soon, daughter, your purpose will be revealed. You must be ready for it," he said. "There is a mind reaper in your midst. You would be wise to trust him. A time will come when he will aid you in your quest."

Then he was gone.

Chapter Twenty-three

River

*M*y room, which had never been all that large, felt even smaller now. I paced back and forth like a caged animal while I waited for Tyler to get off the phone with his dad. The one good thing about having a dad on the force was being able to guilt-trip him for information when we needed it. Something Tyler always did with flying colors.

Today, I asked him to do me a solid and get some background info on Logan. Not exactly what Billie requested of me, but it was a good move as far as I was concerned. That guy was hiding something.

Even though he explained why he'd kept being able to remember Morgan and Lorelei from us, I still didn't trust him. His half-baked excuse for lying about it didn't help either. *Worried about our reaction, my ass!* I understood wanting to stay under the radar more than most people, but the idiot could see how stressed Billie was and still chose not to come forward. What kind of person did that? The cowardly, lying kind. And why tell us the truth later?

Logan was up to no good, and I was going to prove it.

For all we knew, he pretended to remember people just to screw with us.

"Thanks, Dad," Tyler said, and my heart rate sped up. "I owe you one."

When my friend hung up the phone and looked at me, I almost lunged for him. Actually, I pretty much did. My feet carried my body over to tower over him, and I tapped my sneaker against the baseboard to calm down. "What did he say? Did he find something? It's not good, is it? I fucking knew it!"

"Dude," Tyler breathed out and held up a hand, "chill."

I grunted, taking a step back. "Sorry. So, what's the deal?"

The uneasy smile Tyler forced out did not make me want to chill at all. His hands fumbled as he pocketed his cellphone and he refused to meet my eyes. Whatever Tyler's dad uncovered was going to make me freak the hell out. Tyler knew it, and I knew it too.

"Please, tell me before I lose it," I begged.

"Okay, so there's good news and bad news."

"Isn't there always?"

Tipping his weight, Tyler chuckled and leaned back on the mattress. The way his eyes darted left to right made me realize that even the good news in this situation would not be all that great. *Wonderful.*

Frustrated, I backed away, putting some distance between us. Maybe getting out of his face was a better move here. I breathed heavily, urging myself not to shoot the messenger, no matter how much my wolf wanted to lash out at that moment. After a few deep breaths, it seemed to work, and I could carry on a normal conversation without losing my cool. At least, I hoped I did.

"I guess start with the good news," I said.

Tyler's eyebrows kissed and he rubbed the back of his neck. "Well, the guy's name *is* Logan Green, so he wasn't lying about that part."

"Cool," I bit out. "What's the bad news?"

"He's got some sordid shit in his past."

My head pounded and I leaned against my dresser to keep steady. Eyes narrowing on my friend, I clenched my jaw and cracked my neck. "Is he dangerous?"

"Not according to his files. My dad couldn't get much since it's out of his jurisdiction. Long story short, Logan is from a small town in England. Castle Combe or something like that. I guess the guy had a pretty crap life back there. He grew up in foster care until he was permanently taken in when he was eight. The couple that took him in wasn't the best, at least the dad wasn't. There are reports of abuse for a few years, and then it goes dark for a while. My dad dug more and found out that Logan's foster dad died in his home when Logan was eleven. The cops suspected Logan, but after a long investigation, they cleared him. He was placed back in foster care but then escaped. There's no trace of him after that. My dad thinks Logan stayed under the radar until he could move here somehow."

Blood rushed from my face and my heart dropped to my feet. "How did his foster dad die?"

"Brain aneurism. But there were signs of a struggle, which was why they suspected Logan until they did an autopsy."

Shitshitshit! Logan was a mind reaper, and if his dad died of a brain aneurism, there was a good chance it wasn't an accident. This was such a damn mess!

"Why the hell would he run away if they cleared him?" I asked.

Tyler sighed. "I don't know, small town, I guess. People talk. I doubt anyone would want to take him in after that."

"Yeah, no one wants to help a freaking killer."

"Well, according to the files, he wasn't one."

I rolled on my heels, arching an eyebrow. "Dude, come on! The guy is a reaper! Of course, he did it."

"I don't know," Tyler said, looking down at his feet. "Sounds like his foster dad deserved it."

While that was true, it didn't make me feel much better. Logan didn't tell us about his past, so what else was he not telling us? The guy was a liar, and I didn't believe one word that came out of his mouth. The real problem was that I was the only one that felt this way and convincing the others would be difficult at best. Convincing Billie and Savannah would be nearly impossible. Who the hell keeps something like this to themselves? We all have skeletons in our closets, but this was some serious shit. Maybe Logan thought we'd see him differently if we knew? Still, he should have told us.

You're being a hypocrite, I told myself. *This is his life, not yours. Give it a rest.*

I couldn't.

This guy, this possible murderer, was too close to my friends. And way too close to Billie for my liking.

Reaching for my phone, I typed out a message and stared at the screen. In front of me, Tyler's face paled and his shoulders rode up on his thick frame. "What you doin'?"

"Telling Billie what you found out. She needs to know who we're dealing with here," I answered. "Logan had nothing concrete to tell me when I questioned him about remembering Morgan and Lorelei, and I don't trust him around Billie or Savannah. Or anyone else we know."

"Bro, don't you think you're overreacting?"

"No."

My phone buzzed, and I tore my gaze from Tyler to read Billie's message, instantly wishing I didn't. A growl vibrated in my chest and my fingers tightened around the cellphone until I thought I might snap it in two. Shaking, I shoved the phone back into my jean pocket.

"She's cool with it, isn't she?" Tyler asked.

I nodded.

"Well, there you have it! Now, you can move on. Give the guy a break and let's worry about this spell Billie's chasing instead."

Listening to Tyler was the right reaction here, but I couldn't bring myself to do it. Logan was dangerous, and I couldn't understand how Billie trusted someone with such a sordid past. It didn't make any sense to me. After everything we found out, she should have been fuming like I was. Instead, she sided with this shifty moron without a second thought.

Her text replayed in my mind as I tried to focus on anything but Logan. *Leave it alone. Everyone has a past, and this is his secret to keep. I'm sure there's a reason he didn't tell us.*

There sure as shit was a reason for it. He was a damn killer.

Before me, Tyler rose to stand, and his wide shoulders obliterated my view of the bed. "Wanna get out of here?" he asked, turning for the door.

"And go where?"

Tyler wiggled his eyebrows in a way that made me think nothing good could come out of what he was about to say next.

"It's Saturday," he huffed out. "Let's take a day to relax. We could use it. The girls are at the quarry, I say we break up the party."

The last thing on my list of things to do right now was to relax, but Tyler had a point. If Billie would not be reasonable, I would make her see logic. And I couldn't do that over text. I needed to talk some sense into the stubborn girl before her blind trust in Logan landed us in more trouble. I wasn't sure why I was so dead set on making everyone mistrust the reaper. Whatever it was, I had to follow through. There was too much happening around us we couldn't control—people freaking vanishing, the High Coven gunning for Savannah—we didn't need another problem to add to the mix. If we were going to figure out what the hell was going on in Shadowhurst, we couldn't do it with a traitor in our midst.

Deep down, the wolf urged me to calm my shit and I mentally slapped his worry away. Logan was a problem. One I had to get rid of before it was too late.

Chapter
Twenty-four

Billie

My boyfriend was a freaking lunatic. There was really no better way to say it. It was bad enough Peyton dragged me to the quarry for a girls' day when we were in the middle of a damn catastrophe. But now I had to deal with River's crazy fixation on Logan's past? That wasn't happening. I mean, sure, what he told me about the reaper's childhood wasn't great. Actually, it was far from great. But let's be honest here, did anyone else in our group have a perfect childhood? Probably not. I sure as shit didn't, so who was I to judge Logan for not telling us his entire life story? It wasn't as though we were close to him. Except for Savannah, of course, and I doubted even she knew of his history. Whatever reasons Logan had for keeping it from us, I understood. This was his mess to deal with, his darkness, and it wasn't our place to drag it out of him. If anything, the whole thing made it clearer why he didn't tell us about remembering Morgan and Lorelei.

If I was running from my past, I'd have kept my mouth shut too.

I just couldn't understand why River didn't get that. It was like he was set on getting rid of Logan when he should have been worrying about the messed-up situation we were in instead.

Idiot boys.

No matter what River may have thought he knew, I wasn't falling for it. The shadow man told me to trust the reaper in our circle, and now more than ever, I knew he was talking about Logan. Which was likely a stupid idea since I wasn't even sure I could trust the shadow man either, but still. Logan had done nothing to warrant River's craziness, and I was willing to give him the benefit of the doubt. For now.

Rolling the pendant River gave me over my fingers, I stretched out my legs and let my feet graze the water at the edge of the beach. The quarry was blissful this afternoon. The sun heated the cool air and beat down on the crystal water, rippling its rays across the surface. Massive rock walls encased me on either side, and I buried my heels into the sand with a smile. With summer far behind us, the once-popular swimming area was completely abandoned and sitting here now, it felt as though this place existed only for me and my friends.

As much as I hated to admit it, Peyton might have had a point. I really needed this today.

"This is nice," I said, leaning my back against Peyton's. "Good suggestion."

My best friend laughed against me and tossed a bag of chips over her shoulder. It landed in my lap, and I greedily opened it, pouring the contents into my mouth.

"Um, learn to share much?" Savannah scoffed, rolling her eyes at Abigail.

Peyton tossed another bag on Savannah's lap and shook her head. "Share that," she said. "Last one left."

Annoyed, Savannah opened the bag, offering it to Abigail first. When the brunette grimaced in disgust and went back to applying her seventeenth coat of lip gloss, Savannah turned to Mel. "Want some?"

The shifter turned to her side, her eyes drifting over the water. I was still surprised that she tagged along, but Peyton had grown close to the leader since her time at the resistance house, and I had to hand it to Mel, she was kind of awesome to hang out with. Much like myself, she didn't take anyone's shit and it was a blast watching her and Savannah argue. Her presence in our group made me relax, despite the hole in my stomach the memory of the other two girls left behind. Without Morgan and Lorelei, the group seemed incomplete, and my heart broke each time I thought about it.

Two missing.

Two gone.

Two lost.

Twisting around, I nudged Peyton's shoulder and rearranged my seat to face the other girls. "I talked to Vic yesterday," I blurted out, catching them off guard. "About the spell."

Everyone's eyes landed on me, pinning me in place.

"Ugh," Abigail said. "I thought this was chill day."

"In Shadowhurst? Unheard of."

Peyton chuckled and shoved another chip in her mouth while Mel barely registered my words.

"Anyway, I think it has something to do with the days people are born on. And the blood moon. I was thinking we could check to see if my theory is right."

"And how do we do that?" Savannah asked.

Lips curling, I focused my attention on the hunter. "What's your birthday?"

"March twenty-second."

"Aries," I whispered. "Fire sign. Two thousand and three, right?"

Face paling, Savannah cringed at my words. "Yep. Why?"

Not bothering to answer, I typed a search on my phone to pull up the moon schedule for the year she was born. Scanning the results, my chest tightened as I read and when I looked up at Savannah, I could tell my worry had transferred to the group. The hunter's eyes widened, and she drummed her manicured nails on her knees, waiting for me to speak.

I wished I could swallow my tongue.

Reluctantly, I put the phone down and stared at her. "The night you were born, it was a blood moon. Just as I thought."

"Cool!" Abigail hollered. "Do me next!"

"It's not a game," Mel bit out, finally saying something. I was waiting for her to keep talking, but after an awkward moment of silence, the shifter twisted to turn away from us.

Well, that's helpful.

"Wait," Peyton said. "You're serious? This could be a thing?"

I sighed. "Unfortunately, yes. I think the High Coven is taking people born under a blood moon and using their elemental energies to create portals somehow."

"Okay, but why me?" Savannah asked. "Or this Morgan person? Or Lorelei or whatever?"

"I don't know," I admitted.

Beside us, Mel rolled her muscled body again and let out

an exasperated groan. Her thick legs crossed as she sat up and she leaned over, revealing way too much of her cleavage. "Obviously it's to hurt you," she announced.

"Huh?" we all asked in unison.

The shifter brushed back her purple locks and leaned on her elbows. "The coven has it out for you. If it was me, I'd target anyone you know just to make the sting worse."

Eyes wide, the girls looked from me to Mel, and a lump formed in my throat.

"That's actually a pretty good point," Peyton said. "So, how do we check the rest of the dates? No one here knows who the hell these missing girls were."

My heart shattered for my best friend.

"Morgan's an air sign and she was a blood moon baby too," I said. "I already checked. Lorelei, I have no clue. She wasn't exactly easy to get to know and we weren't close."

"Who was she close with?"

"Marcus."

Next to Savannah, Abigail braided her hair tightly. "Awesome, dead end. Shouldn't you check the rest of us just in case? I'm October fifteenth, two thousand two."

"Girl, are you older than me?" Peyton shrieked. "You're like a freaking adult and shit."

The two laughed, though I found it hard to join in. While they were joking around, I searched for Abigail's birthdate in the moon calendar and came up empty. Relief flooded my system and my shoulders relaxed. "You're safe. Peyton too, I checked her last night."

"Bummer," Peyton said, and my eyebrows shot up. "What? Blood moon sounds creepy. I kinda love it."

"You wouldn't if you saw what I saw," Savannah scoffed,

darkness forming behind her eyes. "Whatever those bitches are up to, it hurts like hell."

Memories of the bright light that held her flashed before me and I shook them away. "What about you, Mel?"

The shifter squirmed in her seat and zipped up her red leather jacket.

"September third," she answered. "And I'm definitely not telling you the year."

"Come on!" I begged. "This is important."

I was met with a death glare that made me shrink in my spot. "Ugh, fine!" Mel exclaimed. "It's nineteen—"

Loud steps echoed behind us, and we swung around in a choreographed panic. My jaw hit the sand and I didn't have to see my friends to know their expressions matched mine. As I took in our intruder, my mood shifted between cheer and fear, and I didn't know how to handle it. Before me, Vic's small feet pounded the sand as she marched toward us, yet it wasn't her that gave me pause.

What I couldn't stop watching were the figures trailing behind her.

Witches.

Bile rose in my throat, and I sank into the sand, following my friend rushing down the beach with a dozen witches on her tail.

Chapter
Twenty-five

Billie

The witches flanking Vic's side were unlike any I've seen before. They were dipped head to toe in crystals and the smell of mixed herbs rose off their bodies with such intensity, it made my eyes water. Dark dresses floated behind them, and their unruly hair clung atop their heads in an array of webbed styles that made each one look more sinister than the next. A few had pouches hanging off the sashes adorning their hips, and I had no doubt they were full of potions at the ready. Magic swirled around them so bright, it made me gasp. Every step they took to close the distance between us sent shivers up my legs, and I fought the incessant urge to run building up inside of me.

These were nothing like the coven witches I was used to.

The High Coven witches, while powerful, would never flaunt their magic in public this way, which only made these women more dangerous in my eyes. They were unashamedly magical, and anyone that dared expose our craft so bluntly needed to be feared.

Fear was something I had by the pounds at that moment.

Next to me, Peyton's back tensed as we watched Vic and her crew creep closer to us. From where I sat, I could sense the panic in my best friend. I reached for her hand, offering a light squeeze to reassure her. I wasn't sure what I was trying to prove. I was as scared as she was.

"The hell..." Mel said behind me, and I shot a glance her way to keep her quiet. The less talking we did right now, the better.

At least that's what I told myself. My mouth had other plans altogether.

"Vic, who are these people?" I blurted out before I could stop. *Ugh, shut up!* "You brought witches to Shadowhurst?" *Honestly, you're an actual tool.*

Before me, Vic paused and the witches slowed their stride. Her tight ponytail dripped down her shoulder and her lips curled up at the edges. Vic's eyes found me, and I gulped. "They're friends," she announced. "And not the coven's friends."

Trying to wrap my head around what Vic said made my eyeballs hurt. As far as I knew, every witch in the world was a friend of the coven in one capacity or another. Except for me, of course. I was as far from a friend to those evil assholes as one could get. My attention drifted around the witches at Vic's side again, and my mouth gaped. The blatant use of magic in public, their odd outfits, even the way they watched my friends showing no distaste for the company of shadowers and hunters I kept. It all led to only one conclusion.

"Rogue witches," I said in a hushed tone. "You found rogue witches."

"Damn straight I did!" Vic yelped, her smile spreading wider across her face until it was all I could see. She moved to tower over me, and behind her, a few witches floated closer. One by one, they inspected my reaction as though *I* was the one that didn't fit into the equation. When Vic knelt before me, I fought the urge to barf. "What?" she asked, "Did you think we were the only ones who wanted nothing to do with the coven?"

I kind of did. "How did you find them?"

"And how many are there?" Peyton added, stiffening beside me.

"Like I said before, I have friends outside the High Coven. This is them. As for how many, well, let's just say enough."

Acid rose in my throat and my vision blurred. "Enough for what?"

"To take down the coven, of course. When we're ready."

"This chick is batshit." Savannah snickered behind me. "I like it. So, what's the point of bringing them here? No offense, ladies, but we have no clue what we're even dealing with. You're kinda wasting your time on this trip."

One rogue witch chuckled, and her voice carried over us and into the water. The rest looked toward me with such intensity, I had to bury my fingers into the sand to keep from screaming. Despite what Savannah thought, no one here wasted their time. They knew something, something I was sure I wouldn't enjoy hearing. Tentatively, I peered past Vic's shoulder and grimaced. "I'm guessing this will not be news we want to hear?"

"Depends on what you're looking for," the witch who laughed said. I focused on her face, gaze drifting over her freckled skin and settling on the amber eyes that pierced through me. She was older, well into her fifties, with a seriousness to her demeanor that entrapped me. I could tell that whoever this rogue witch was, she'd seen enough in her lifetime to fill in the gaps for us. Anticipation clawed at my chest, and I leaned over my knees as the witch continued to speak. "My name is Catarina," she said, eyes never leaving mine. "Victoria had assured my sisters and me that you have no loyalty to the High Coven. I am hopeful that is still the case."

"It is," I choked out.

"Damn straight," Peyton scoffed. The rest of our friends nodded.

The witch, Catarina, moved to stand behind Vic, her wide frame blocking out the sun above us. "We have little time. According to Victoria, the coven was successful in establishing a portal, correct?"

"Unfortunately, yes. Do you know how they did that?"

Catarina ran her tongue over her teeth and crossed her arms. The crystals sewn into the sleeve of her dress jingled, and I got a whiff of lavender when she moved. "I do. How much do you know about the High Coven's initiation rituals for junior witches?"

"Um," I said, biting the inside of my cheek, "just that it has to happen on a full moon and witches share their magic when it goes down to welcome the new member. It's a pretty sweet ritual, actually. I kind of miss it."

"You won't when you hear this," Vic hissed under her breath. "Catarina, tell her what the ritual is really for."

What the heck does that mean?

"When a new witch is initiated into the coven," Catarina continued, giving me zero room to ask questions, "the other witches involved do in fact share power. What they don't tell you, the vile creatures, is where all that magic goes. The high priestesses have been siphoning magic from initiated witches for years. Harboring it for later use."

"Wait, what?" Mel asked. "They're stealing magic from their coven members?"

"Correct."

The shifter's back uncurled and her forehead scrunched. "Why?"

"We're not entirely certain," Catarina answered. "We are assuming they're doing so to strengthen their magic for spells that require more power than they have on their own. The high priestesses are strong, but their magic is limited, much like the rest of ours. Even with the head witches helping, there are spells out there they could not cast with their magic alone."

"Why not just ask the coven for help?" I inquired. "I'm sure every witch under their rule would have no problem offering their magic willingly. Why steal it?"

Catarina's lips twitched.

"Because what the High Coven told you about the limited power a junior witch possesses is a lie. Young witches are not as weak as they want you to believe, at least not at the beginning. They are incredibly strong because their magic is unregulated. Think of them as brand new cars, all the horsepower without the mileage. New witches are as close to original magic as one can get. We assume that the high priestesses are taking all this untapped magic before it is weakened by a lifetime of use. While, over time, a witch can hone her magic and become more practiced in the ways of using it, nothing compares to the energy your blood has when you first come into your powers."

"So, hang on here," I bit out. "You're telling me that every witch in the coven was way stronger before the initiation?"

"Yes."

"I don't understand. Why not let them keep their magic? Coven witches are loyal to a fault, wouldn't it make sense for the high priestesses to ask them for help instead of taking their powers?"

"You would think so, yes," Catarina mused. "Except that would lessen the control the coven has over all of you. It is much easier to take someone's power than it is to convince them to part with it. The high priestesses know how to wield the coven to their benefit, they have for years. And I'm not speaking only of the women you know today. This has been happening long before our time and will continue to happen unless we do something about it."

"Not to sound like a total moron," Abigail interrupted, "but I still don't get what they're doing with all this extra magic. Like, where are they keeping it? In a jar or something?"

"What she said," Peyton agreed.

The rogue witches exchanged glances before turning back to face us. Their feet shuffled the sand, shifting the weight of their bodies and triggering all my nerves at once. "You don't know, do you?" I asked.

"No, we do not. Somehow, the High Coven found a way to siphon the magic of young witches as soon as they come into their power. How they did this and where the magic is going is not something we've been able to uncover. One of us came close, but it didn't pan out."

"What happened to her?"

A glimmer of sadness flashed behind Catarina's eyes and when she looked down at me, my heart tore at the edges. The rogue witch ran a finger through her hair, resting her hand on my shoulder and squeezing to get my full attention. "For years, those of us that didn't agree with the coven's way of doing things fled. We didn't believe their lies about the shadowers, having realized all too late that it was all a ploy to erase their own mistakes. We believed the ruthless ruling of the high priestesses even less. Even before Sebyl and her sisters, the high priestesses held witches by their throats, forcing them to follow rules that some of us did not want to follow.

"Years ago, a young witch gave birth to a daughter, and much like everyone else, she fell in line. As her daughter grew, the witch's eyes opened to the evil ways of the coven until she could no longer take it. She fought against the priestesses and their head witches, battling them in every way in hopes of righting the corruption in the coven. It was a pointless task. One that cost her more than it should have.

"Upon finding out that other witches felt as she had, the woman sought us out. She was the one that discovered the truth about the initiations, and when she realized her daughter would undergo the same treatment, she was determined to bring it to an end. So, we worked with her. The witch continued to report to the coven, all the while feeding us information from the inside. One night, she sent a message letting us know she was onto a lead. One that was going to tell us what the priestesses were doing with the magic they siphoned from junior witches. But things went wrong. Very, very wrong. The high priestesses discovered her betrayal, and after that, there was no way for us to contact her again."

My face blanched. "What did they do with her?"

"They trapped her in the magical prison, and the high priestesses took it upon themselves to raise her daughter. A final stab to guarantee her silence."

Every cell in my body vibrated as the story fell from

Catarina's lips. My mind raced and my pulse drummed under my skin, drowning out all other sounds in the quarry. The high priestesses took in only one witch I knew of, and the thought shattered me into pieces.

"The witch you're talking about," I murmured. "It was Beatrix. It was my mom."

Catarina's gaze dropped to the sand. "Yes."

There was no time for my world to explode. Before I could press the rogue witch further, voices lapped the beach and my feet hit the sand, propelling me to stand. My eyes shot from the rogue witches to the furthest point of the quarry, and my thundering heart leaped into my throat. Head pounding, I watched as figures appeared on the horizon and warm saliva pooled under my tongue.

SHIT.

Chapter Twenty-six

River

*B*illie's face watching me approach the quarry said it all. She was not expecting to see me here. I wish I could say I felt bad for barging in on her party, but when I saw Victoria and the dozen witches surrounding my girl, I stopped caring pretty quickly.

What is going on here?

In my gut, my wolf kicked against my psyche and growled like a wild animal. *I know, dude, I'm freaking out too.* Pushing him away, I marched down the beach to get closer to Billie, whose face paled by the second as I approached. Beside me, Jayden and Tyler puffed their chests while Griffin growled through his teeth. No one liked what was happening, and I couldn't blame my friends for being on high alert. This many witches was bad news.

Scanning the women, I turned my gaze to Billie, trying to understand why she remained so calm in their midst. *What are you doing, babe? Attack them!* When Billie did nothing but stare at me, my confusion deepened, forcing me to look back to the witches. There was so much off about them.

Mostly though, it was that they didn't have the self-assured, evil faces of the High Coven, and as much as I looked, I couldn't spot the high priestesses anywhere. Was there a chance these witches weren't part of the coven? *No way. That's unheard of. Isn't it?*

When we finally reached Billie, my brain was on fire.

"Babe? What's this?" I asked, picking my words carefully. "You okay?"

Blood rushed back to her face and when she brushed a shoulder against mine, I felt every tense muscle in my body loosen. Tearing my attention from her, I turned to Victoria. "Someone want to explain this to me?"

"River," Billie said, "meet the rogue witches."

"The what and the who now?" Jayden asked, his pitch rising. "Rogue witches? Serious?"

"It just keeps getting better, huh?" Savannah teased. I found nothing about this situation funny.

Head jerking right and left, I tried to memorize every face before me like I was going to pick them out of a lineup later. The witches watched me with the same intensity, amplifying the pallor beneath my tanned skin. Their eyes dropped to my fisted hands, and I worked to uncurl my fingers to ease the awkwardness. Unfortunately for everyone on the beach, my wolf didn't have the same resolve and instead of relaxing, I ended up growling like a fool instead. *Fabulous.*

At my side, Billie brushed a finger against my fist and nudged my ribs. "Stand down, soldier. They're friends."

"I don't think so," Griffin bit out.

I filled my lungs, letting out the slowest breath possible before casting a side glance in his direction. "Let's hear her out."

While Tyler and Jayden took little convincing, it was a few strenuous moments until Griffin stepped down and followed my lead. Even from here, I could sense his anger toward the witches and I couldn't blame him. Griffin had been a shadower a hell of a lot longer than me, so I knew his experience with witches was less than friendly. I wondered how many of his friends got vanquished by the High Coven. Even one was too many.

Still, the women standing before us didn't seem like a threat and Billie trusted them, Victoria too, which was enough to give me pause.

Shifting my weight, I focused on Billie. "Fill us in, I guess."

"They're going to help us take the coven down. The High Coven has been siphoning magic from junior witches for years, and Catarina intends to stop it. Oh, and I think they can help us figure out the whole blood moon spell, though I haven't asked yet cause you dorks showed up and interrupted," she said, sticking her tongue out at me. "And they know my mom."

Blasted hell, babe! You lead with the mom thing! "... Okay," I choked out.

"Blood moon spell?" one rogue witch, Catarina I assumed, asked.

Whispers broke out around us as the other witches raised their questions. Their voices carried over the quarry, each one landing a new blow to Billie until I swore I could see her buckle back from their raised concerns. If they didn't shut up soon, she was going to lose it. My fists tightened again, and I let out a low hiss, which seemed to shut some women up.

"We're not here for problems, shifter," Catarina said. I

should have been insulted, annoyed at least, but her voice was calm and measured so I let the words drip off me. "What is your name?"

"River."

"Ladies," the rogue witch shouted over the other women, "this is River. He and these boys are of no threat to us. Any friend of Victoria and Billie is an ally of ours." She nodded at my friends, then faced Billie. "The blood moon spell you mentioned, what is it?"

Man, she's good, I thought as I watched the other witches settle down in seconds.

"People have been getting erased around town, friends of ours," Billie said. "I think the High Coven is working some spell that is making them disappear. They were after Savannah last time and hit her with some light magic that messed with her memories. I believe this is what they used to grab the others and delete them from everyone's mind."

"These people," Catarina mused, "they were born under a blood moon, yes? Each one with a different elemental sign?"

"Yes. So, you think I'm right?"

"I don't think," the rogue witch said harshly. "I know. There is only one spell I can think of that could create this illusion, one your mother knew well, as a matter of fact. It is powerful magic and requires a lot of strength to achieve. To alter the memory of this many people, the coven must have cast an illusion over the entire town. A bubble of magic, if you will. An illusion on this large a scale would guarantee that anyone who is within the town's perimeter when the spell is cast only sees what the coven wills them to see. Essentially, they have created an alternate reality, a memory that exists only as they summoned it." Catarina inhaled and burrowed her eyes into mine. "One agreement we had with Beatrix was for her to deliver spells to us that might aid in fighting against the coven. This spell was in that mix. It is quite powerful, and if the priestesses are willing to cast it, there is a big enough return guaranteed."

"Where did she find this spell?" Billie asked.

Catarina paused. "I'm not sure. Some old grimoire she found in the coven's library."

So that's why that head witch wanted the Book of Darkness. To make sure we never get our hands on what they might be up to. I seriously hated the coven in that moment. Every muscle in my jaw twitched. "What kind of return are we talking about? For the spell, I mean."

"One we do not wish to have them achieve. If the portal they arrived in is any indication, I would bet they are attempting to use the blood moon spell to create another portal. One that is far greater than the one you witnessed."

"Well, that was pretty freaking great," I growled out. "What's bigger than that thing?"

Catarina's face fell and her lips turned downward. "A portal between worlds."

Another wave of whispers surrounded us, and this time, I joined in the commotion. I had no clue what a portal between worlds meant, but I had a feeling it couldn't be anything good. Were there even other worlds out there? I didn't know, and I didn't wish to find out.

"Okay, back it up, guys," Jayden yelped. "Are you seriously telling me there's another world? What kind of world? Is it magical? Are there sirens in it? Please, tell me there are sirens!"

A loud slap sounded over his annoying exclaims and when I turned, I saw Savannah crack her knuckles and a red mark spread over the exposed skin on Jayden's chest. Leave it to my best friend to slap a guy when he's spiraling.

"Not cool, girlfriend," Jayden yelped and rubbed his chest. "Not cool at all."

"But very needed," Sav said with a smirk.

Fighting the chuckle about to burst from my lips, I peeled my gaze from them to focus on Billie. Her eyes were wider than moons and I could see her brain working a million miles a minute. She was trying to process this the same way we all were, except in her case, it likely went far deeper. I couldn't imagine what this was like for her. To find out she was right all along was one thing, but to hear it from witches that knew her mother was a whole new ball game. She must have been tearing herself inside out right now. Though I knew there was nothing I could say to make it better, I tried regardless.

I leaned into her, my lips grazing her ears. "This is good," I said low enough for only her to hear. "It means your mom wasn't as bad as you thought."

If she heard me, she didn't register it and my heart plummeted. More than anything, I wanted to fix this for her, but now was not the time for that.

Damn this town to Hell!

"This portal you're talking about," Billie said, "where does it lead?"

"I'm not sure," Catarina answered. "Wherever it is, we cannot let them succeed. If we've learned anything from the High Coven's actions, it's that they do not serve any other purpose than to gain power. Power we cannot allow them to have. Your mother risked her life going against them, we will not let her sacrifice go in vain."

"You're talking about her like she's dead," Billie sniped. "Don't."

"I apologize," Catarina drawled. "Beatrix was a good friend of mine, of all of ours. We will do what is required to finish what she started. You have our word."

Snaking an arm around her waist, I pulled Billie into me. Her body shook against me, but every time she threatened to break away, I strengthened my hold. Whether or not she realized it, Billie needed me right now and I would not let her think she was in this alone. After a few moments, her tension melted, and a smile spread over my face.

I got you.

The rogue witch watched us with interest, studying the way I clung to Billie and the way she allowed me to continue. Her lips tightened into a thin line, and I wondered if she was fighting the urge to tell us off the same way Sebyl did whenever she saw us together. If this woman so much as breathed the wrong way, I would tear her throat out.

To my surprise, Catarina did no such thing. Her amber eyes brightened and she peeled her gaze from the arm I held around Billie's mid-section to look at my girlfriend. "It's strange you can remember the people the coven is taking. Can the rest of you?"

All of us shook our heads 'no' while Billie stiffened in my arms.

"Only me," she said. "Well, me and one other person, but he's not here."

"Very interesting indeed." Catarina's chin lifted and she looked past us to the water's edge. Her brows furrowed like she was struggling to put pieces together that didn't quite fit, and at that moment, I would have given anything to read the witch's mind.

"Dudes and dudettes," Jayden said loud enough to make everyone jump. "Where did we land on the whole sirens thing?"

Beside him, Savannah raised a hand to hit him once more, but before she could make contact, a bright blue light flashed in my peripheral vision. Her hand dropped and my best friend's eyes met mine only seconds before the light expanded, covering the entire quarry in its glow. The army of rogue witches twirled on their heels to face it. The hunters reached for their weapons. The shadowers spread their feet wide and got ready to use their powers.

I should have been doing the same.

I didn't.

All I could do was look down at Billie and watch as her jaw clicked at the sight of a portal opening on the beach and the high priestesses emerge from it.

Chapter Twenty-seven

Billie

*E*ven before River's nails dug into my skin, I felt the magic of the High Coven in the air. Seeing the blue glow of the opening portal was just the cherry on top of a very shitty, very horrifying cake.

This is the worst time for this.

Actually, wait, now is a perfect time.

While the high priestesses and head witches piled out of their stupid portal like clowns exiting a tiny car, I kept my eyes on the rogue witches. For once, we had something the coven didn't expect. Backup.

"Everyone get back!" River yelled over my shoulder. "Stay together!"

Our friends huddled behind me while the rogue witches took the front, magic swirling in colorful patterns on their fingertips. I reached for my own, forgetting for a second that I was a useless pile of garbage these days. *Thanks, maybe-dad! Excellent timing with the whole taking my magic away thing. Real wonderful.*

A shoulder pressed into mine and River's woodsy scent

washed over me. "Don't do anything rash, babe. Let them handle this." He may as well have been miming because I was not about to listen to any of that nonsense.

Before River could hold me back, I leaped from his side to join Catarina at the front. My skin tingled from being so close to her magic, to all of theirs. Rogue witches on either of my side made my confidence jump to a hundred, and even without magic of my own, I swore I was stronger.

The portal pulsed and my eyes narrowed.

A gleam of blue grabbed my attention, carrying my gaze to Theodora's teased hair behind a line of head witches. Her hands held massive amethysts and the energy she pulled from the crystals shone a brilliant purple in her palms. At her side, Rhiamon and Luna worked glowing balls of fire each and when they took a step inward. I shivered.

"River! Cover Savannah, they're coming in hot!"

Not bothering to look behind me, I struggled to connect to the amber crystal sewn into Catarina's leather belt, but nothing happened. *Crap!* My mind raced as a fireball zoomed by me and straight for the rogue witches. A hand grabbed my shoulder and yanked me around, pushing me away from the blast. I spun on my heels to see Catarina shield me with her body and blast Luna with a fireball of her own.

It missed.

Of course, it missed.

Magic rushed all around me and screams tore from the rogue witches as they fought against the attacks. In my peripheral vision, I saw a few hit the ground, their bodies still as night. This day would end in bloodshed if we didn't think of something soon. My gaze tore through the quarry, landing on River and the shifters. "We need help!"

Not missing a beat, River dropped to all fours with Griffin and Mel following suit. I fought the urge to keep staring as their bones reformed and the sounds of clothes tearing rose over the screams. In mere seconds, two wolves and a lioness stood in place of my friends, their eyes glowing bright and their canines bared.

A fierce lightning bolt rolled by me, and I hissed as its electric current sliced my cheek. Whipping my palm to the stinging wound, I snapped my head toward my attacker and my stomach dropped. Close to where I stood, Rhiamon's lips parted into a wide mouth grin and her eyes narrowed, beckoning me forward. *Goddess help me.* Fury burned my throat, and I widened my stance, bluffing confidence. *She doesn't know you can't use your magic. Fake it 'til you make it. Fake it good.*

Pressing closer to the rogue witches at my side, I flattened my palms, stretching my arms outward. Begging for a miracle, I reached for their unprotected crystals and closed my eyes. A rumble vibrated my chest as I battled my imprisoned magic, willing it to be free. It fought against me and no matter how hard I tried, my body remained my own.

Freaking HELL!

Even from this far away, I could sense Rhiamon's smile widen as she realized I was no threat to her.

Another lightning bolt rushed by, and I swerved out of its way just in time. Twisting my body, I stepped into the line of rogue witches protecting us and disappeared from view. My head roared like a car misfiring and angry tears stung the back of my eyes. On every side of me, magic whirled as coven witches blasted us with their power. The ground shook and I watched in awe as Catarina and three of her friends worked the sand to our advantage. They pulled the small grains upward, floating them to the sky and obscuring us in a wall of pale yellow. Commands rose behind the wall; the coven regrouping to attack again. Their magic pounded at the sand, hitting the impenetrable force and bursting to our side, only to be extinguished immediately.

"Catarina!" I yelled out, "They can't get through your magic, we need to keep it up as long as possible!"

"On it!" the rogue witch responded, and motioned for more of her sisters to join her. In unison, their fingers spread, pulling more of the sand into the wall to strengthen its hold. If they could keep this going, we might actually stand a chance.

Huddling together, I inched my body closer to River's wolf, letting the warmth of his gray fur encompass my legs. He let out a low growl and nudged my knee with his wet nose. Steps behind him, Griffin's wolf stood guard, periodically looking to River for guidance.

With the rogue witches working the wall, I took the chance to scan the rest of our friends. Directly behind me, Tyler crouched next to Mel's lioness, her massive body shielding him from the fight. Peyton and Abigail flanked Savannah, whose face was impossible to read. It was trapped somewhere between fear and the need to fight. A feeling I understood all too well. The hunter had no weapons with her, none of us did, but I could see the urge to attack build in her eyes. I hoped she would stand down long enough for us to think of a new plan.

Turning my attention back to Catarina, I took a ragged breath in. "We have to—"

My words caught in my throat as a burst of blue illuminated the quarry from behind us.

Spinning, I twisted away from River and a gasp broke

free of my lips. Only a few feet from us, a gargantuan portal opened and Sebyl's vile face came into view. The priestess wore a navy suit and I noticed each gold button strain under her heavy breaths as she flung her arms outward, blasting wind toward Peyton and Abigail. The girls skidded back, their feet dragging sand, and landed on their behinds, leaving Savannah out in the open.

"NO!" I yelled, rushing toward the hunter with River's wolf at my side.

My legs pumped and I bolted with more speed than I thought I had. It was still not enough.

Before we could get to Savannah, Sebyl's fingers curled, and she wrapped invisible winds around the hunter's middle. Savannah shrieked, her body flailing as the priestess dragged her away from us and into the open portal.

"Savannah!" I shouted.

Each time my boots landed in the sand, the weight of my body sunk further, and I kicked at the ground to speed up. Dust rose around us as we ran, with River howling to beckon Griffin forward. We were almost next to Sebyl when the priestess took a step back and the portal closed around her, leaving us alone in the quarry.

River let out an agonizing howl and I fell to my knees, burying my fingers into the sand. *This can't be happening.*

Behind me, the coven witches continued to throw their magic at the wall.

Why aren't they leaving? They got Savannah, why are they still here?

My eyes met River's and I could see he was thinking the same. "They're not done," I said to him. "Why aren't they done?"

The words were still on the tip of my tongue when the

portal opened again, and a huge fireball shot out from inside. My head followed the fire, jaw unclenching to let out a scream while I watched it pummel Tyler in the chest. He flew back, landing on his back with sand splattering all around him. Abigail ran to his side, throwing her body atop the burning flesh to put it out. Her eyes watered as she swatted at the flames, finally extinguishing them.

When she looked up, my heart shot up in my throat.

"You bitch!" Abigail screamed.

My head turned and my entire body convulsed.

At the edge of the blue light of the portal, Sebyl stood. Her wicked smile spreading and her fingers glittering with magic as she twisted her palms toward Abigail. My friend gasped, clutching her throat and beating at her chest.

"She's pulling the air out of her lungs!" I shouted. "We must stop her!"

I flung myself at Abigail, body checking her away from Tyler to break the hold Sebyl had on her. It seemed to work because when I peeled myself off her chest, her eyes were closed but she was breathing again.

Tears flooded my vision as I dove for Tyler, checking his wounds. Acid burned my mouth when I touched the black marks over his body and panic overtook me. He wasn't moving.

NONONO!

My fingers clasped his nose, and I pressed my lips to his, blowing out air as fast as I could manage. I had never tried to resuscitate someone before, and all I had to go by was whatever I saw in movies. Even as I attempted to breathe life into him over and over again, I knew it was a lost cause. Mascara ran down my face and I sobbed into Tyler's chest. My arms and legs grew cold and my body shook while I cried.

Minutes passed, though they felt like hours. Lifetimes, really. My vision blurred and when someone dragged me away from Tyler, I didn't fight back.

"Someone call nine one one!" River shouted, loud enough to blow my eardrums. "Babe? Babe, look at me!"

I turned to him, my face heated and wet and my entire body convulsing. Mouth filling with vomit, I looked past River's exposed chest to Tyler's stiff body and let out a painful scream.

River's muscular arms encircled me, and I pounded fists into his shoulders. I was so lost in my grief, I didn't notice how quiet the quarry had become. All signs of magic faded away, and when I looked at the spot the portal was only moments ago, it was emptier than my heart.

Choking down spit, I twisted in River's hold. "What happened? Where did she go? I'm going to kill her!"

"She's gone," River said, his voice hushed. "They all are."

My eyes darted over the quarry, looking for any sign of Savannah when I realized someone else was missing. Checking every terrified face, I slumped down, letting my hurt shatter me to pieces.

Mel was gone too.

While I was busy with Tyler, Sebyl must have grabbed her.

A heavy hand squeezed my shoulder, and I didn't bother to look at River again. Didn't bother asking him about Savannah and Mel. The portal was closed, and I knew what would come next.

My friends were already erased.

Chapter Twenty-eight

Billie

Four thousand two hundred and seventy-eight minutes—the exact amount of time that passed since Savannah and Mel disappeared. To say the last three days have been hell would be an understatement.

You'd think after everything that happened, convincing the others that more of our friends disappeared would have been easy. It wasn't. In fact, it was so damn hard, it made my head hurt. Peyton and Vic got on board pretty fast, which did not surprise me. River was an entirely different story. I couldn't even fault him for it. To be honest, I wasn't sure how he was keeping himself together at all.

Not that I fared much better.

Ever since we made it back from the quarry, I spent each second holed up in my room. No one talked on the ride home, no one even made eye contact. Driving through town, River kept his eyes on the road while Peyton and Jayden cradled an inconsolable Abigail in her lap. I stared out the window, unblinking.

One second was all it took to demolish us. One death. One friend snuffed out from existence.

Well, three if you count Savannah and Mel. The others didn't, but I knew better. We didn't just lose Tyler that day. We lost all three of them.

I had seen my fair share of death in my lifetime. Unfortunately, being a witch meant death came with the job. When I was little, Beatrix told me that dying wasn't a tragedy. It was simply a way of moving on. After the High Coven imprisoned her, my life seemed to revolve around people moving on. Whether it was a shadower I vanquished in the coven's name or other witches we lost during patrols, the results were always the same. Someone would not return and I was left with an emptiness in the base of my stomach the size of a football field.

Tyler's death was no different.

The days that followed were a routine I was quite used to. We slept, we woke up, we grieved. It was a cycle I had never learned to break, no matter how many people I lost along the way.

Our parents, or parent-adjacent figures in my case, insisted we stay back from school for the week which was fine by me. Coming back to the academy after such an extreme loss felt like a sham. As though we were all pretending to be fine when we were anything but.

I messaged River several times to check on him but was met with a wall. Again, not his fault. Everyone dealt with death differently, and while he mourned his friend in solitude, I had other plans.

Sure, I was as torn up about Tyler as the others. I had the same nightmares and woke up in the same sweat soaked sheets. The days melted into each other and were as unbearable for me as they were for the rest of my friends. Yet, I knew myself by now and sitting around feeling sorry for myself was not my way of handling the shitstorm life threw our way. Tyler may have been gone, but we had friends out there that needed our help. Friends that were still breathing.

Laying on my bed, I uncurled my fingers from the tight fists I held them in and rubbed the crescent moons my nails left behind in the soft flesh. My eyes bloodshot, I swung my legs over the mattress with a groan, reaching for my cellphone.

The message I sent to River was the same as the ones before. It was so repetitive, I may as well have copy and pasted it into the chat. *Do you want to talk?*

Blue dots flashed on the screen, and I knew what it would say without looking. I looked anyway.

Not right now. I'm with the pack.

Rolling my eyes, I tossed the phone on the bed. "No shock there."

While the rest of us trapped ourselves in the prison of our homes, River did quite the opposite. He spent every damn second in the resistance house with his pack. Don't get me wrong, it relieved me that he had an outlet for his grief, but this was getting ridiculous. Not long ago, he wanted nothing to do with the wolves and now, they had taken up every minute of his every day. Something shifted in the resistance, and though I couldn't put my finger on it, I had a pretty good idea what.

To anyone else, River's sudden interest in the pack would seem like nothing more than a coping mechanism, a way to bond with others like him in his time of need. Yet, that wasn't entirely the case. The resistance had changed in the last few days. Raiden was always angry and the shadowers living under his roof matched his stride. It was as though they fed off the negative energy he projected, and I feared River was doing much the same. His tone was different when he spoke, and he kept a guard around him I couldn't penetrate, no matter how hard I tried.

There was only one explanation for this change, and I hated that I was the only one who knew it.

Mel and Savannah's disappearance from our memories changed everything.

It was the same with Peyton after Morgan vanished. She was still her, but different somehow, like her personality shifted overnight.

With Mel and Savannah gone, everyone was slightly askew. Almost as if a small part of them reformed into new people and it tainted the entire town in return.

Of course, it wasn't everyone that concerned me. My primary worry was River and the person he became overnight.

My eyes watered and for a brief second, Sebyl's face flashed before me. "I'm going to end you, you bitch," I hissed out into my empty bedroom.

Shaking, I reached for the ice cold fries Imala dropped off hours ago and shoved one in my mouth. Saliva pooled around the soggy potato, and I gagged when I forced myself to swallow. As Imala said, I had to eat. I chewed another fry and headed for the bathroom.

Struggling against myself, I splashed water over my puffy face and brushed back the unruly mess that was my hair, scowling the entire time. My eyes met the reflection in the mirror, and I groaned in disgust.

"You're a hot mess," I scolded.

No matter how much I wanted to cry again, I willed the

tears away and pushed away from the counter. Breaking down was not doing me any good. It wasn't doing anyone any good. Shadowhurst was falling apart, and I needed to fix it before it reached a point of no return, but I had no concrete answers. Catarina and the rogue witches had no clue what portal the High Coven was attempting to open was and where they held our friends until it was time to perform the stupid spell remained a mystery. To make matters worse, counting Mel and Savannah, they had four people already. Four elements. In my state of delirium, I figured out Mel's birthday and it was exactly as I thought. She was an earth sign born under a blood moon.

The pulse behind my temples intensified and I bit the inside of my cheek. "You should have watched over her. You should have watched over all of them."

The words were salt on open wounds.

I had spent so much time blaming myself for what happened, I didn't even know what to believe anymore. Catarina said the spell the coven cast to erase my friends was an illusion, and it would take a lot of power to break it. The kicker was that we couldn't break it without finding our friends, and since we had nothing to go on, we were shit out of luck.

My knees buckled and I gripped the marble counter with enough strength to shatter it in half. An entire town covered in an illusion spell. What a freaking disaster.

In the dim-lit bedroom, my phone vibrated and lit up the ceiling in a bright glow. I dove for it, heart racing, hoping to see River's name pop up on the screen. When I read the message, my stomach turned.

It wasn't River.

Hey. Logan's text said as I scrolled down. *I'm sorry about what happened. I know you're probably feeling shite, but I talked to Victoria and we think we should keep working on this.*

I drifted between hope and aggravation while I typed.

Where do you want to start?

While Logan typed a response, I shoved a handful of fries into my mouth and pulled my hair back into a top bun. My clothes reeked of sweat and depression and I wasn't in any state to leave the house, but I doubted Logan or Vic cared for my appearance. Legs still shaking, I swallowed the bitter taste coating my tongue and squared my shoulders.

Four thousand two hundred and seventy-eight minutes was exactly what I needed.

I let the rage fill me as I rose to stand and headed for the door. Whatever illusion the coven cast over this town, I was going to destroy it. Even if it killed me. The high priestesses may have gotten four elements, but they were still missing one. That gave us time. Sure, it wasn't a lot, but it was better than nothing.

With resolve fueling my every step, I shut the door behind me and inhaled the cold air. Fresh pine crawled up my nostrils and the wind whipped at my face as I walked, shivering.

The high priestesses had the town fooled and they might have thought they had us beat, but there was one thing they didn't count on. They trained me to put my crap aside and do what was necessary. They trained me to survive, and that was what I planned on doing.

"Kiss my witch ass, Shadowhurst," I ground out and stepped into the street. "You have no clue who you're dealing with."

Chapter Twenty-nine

River

The woods unfolded before me as I sprinted over the rough terrain, going nowhere in particular. I had shifted hours ago, shedding my human form like soiled clothes. The last text from Billie made my mind race and as much as I wanted to see her and talk to her, I couldn't bring myself to do it. Not when I was like this.

Broken and dangerous.

The wind ruffled my fur, and I pounded the ground with the weight of my wolf, zigging and zagging through the thick foliage of the trees. Above me, the sun did little to warm the air and I could feel the chill penetrate deep into my bones. I let out a howl, listening for the others to respond. Their voices roared to meet me, and my muscles tensed, knowing the pack was nearby. We had been out here for days, running and hunting and letting our animal counterparts go wild. Well, the pack was hunting. I was doing pretty much anything I could to keep from thinking.

That was why I didn't see Billie. Because she wanted to talk and talking was the last thing on my list right now.

Every time I closed my eyes, I saw the paramedics load the gurney holding Tyler's dead body into the back of the ambulance. I saw his lifeless eyes. Heard Abigail's screams. Watched helplessly while Jayden rubbed his bloodshot eyes and refused to meet my gaze.

Tyler was our friend, our best friend, and nothing would be the same without him. He was the one that always kept his shit together while the rest of us freaked out, the reason for me not losing it each time something out of my control happened. Without him, all I wanted was to set the world on fire.

How was I supposed to explain that to Billie?

I couldn't.

Not that our friend's death didn't affect her, I was certain it did, but it couldn't have caused her this much pain. She didn't know Tyler as I did. Didn't consider him family. Even after his death, when she texted me to check in, I knew her mind was elsewhere. It was caught up in the people she said went missing during the fight, the friends no one but her remembered. I could tell she wanted to discuss it, and the mere idea of having to discuss someone I couldn't even picture revolted me. There was no way in hell that I could worry about two girls I didn't know when Tyler's death robbed me of sanity. Billie didn't get it, so I left.

And I went to the only place I knew would offer an escape.

The pack didn't ask why I returned after so much time spent avoiding them. Instead, they welcomed me with open arms. They allowed me to join their runs, and though the first time was unbearably awkward, I learned to put the thoughts away and enjoy being out with others of my kind.

It was peaceful, for the most part.

A branch snapped near to me, and I skidded in my path, twisting my body to face the sound. I should have been on higher guard, but it seemed stupid to do so. If anyone wanted to take me on now, they had another think coming to them.

My glowing eyes scanned the forest, lighting the area before me in a bright shade of green. A few more twigs crunched underfoot, and I tilted my head to the side to watch Raiden part the trees. His jaw set and his arms crossed at the chest as he took a few more steps forward.

"Mind shifting?" the resistance leader asked, tossing a fresh shirt and slacks on the ground next to my paws.

I growled but did as he asked.

When I dressed, I leaned on a thick tree trunk and buried a foot into the bark. "Any particular reason you're interrupting my run?"

"Just thought you could use a break," Raiden said.

"Peyton sent you, didn't she?"

There was no need for Raiden to answer, I knew as much was true. Peyton had been keeping tabs on me, for Billie, no doubt, ever since the quarry. Much like me, she had taken to spending more time at the house with the other shadowers, and I enjoyed seeing her take her role as a leader seriously. Unlike before, when she whined and complained each time a shadower needed something, Peyton was different now. More assertive and more pissed. I liked it.

I lowered into a crouch and looked up at Raiden. "You guys don't have to keep checking on me," I bit out. "I'm fine."

"Clearly," Raiden said. I didn't appreciate the sarcasm. "When's the funeral?"

My pulse drummed and my head grew foggy. "Sunday," I answered, swallowing down the vile taste that filled my mouth. "Assuming you'll be there?"

"Of course. We all will."

"Good. That's good," I said. *There is nothing good about any of this.* "Can I ask you a question?"

Raiden's lips parted into a sly grin. "Shoot."

"Think I should talk to Billie? I've been pushing her away and I feel like a prick for it."

The lion shifter rubbed his bald head while he considered my words. His massive chest rose and fell under deep breaths and his feet shifted the heavy weight of his body, making him sway like a pendulum. After a few moments, he shoved his hands in his pockets and found my eyes again. "I don't think I'm the best person to give relationship advice," he said. "Lifetime bachelor over here, remember?"

Something about the way he said made my stomach turn, but I couldn't put my finger on what was bothering me. Choosing not to add any more stress to the day, I tucked the worries away and pulled myself to stand.

"Okay, but let's say that wasn't the case and you weren't such a bastard," I suggested. "Would you go talk to her if you were me?"

"Probably not."

What? "For real?"

"I mean, yeah, man. Your girl should be the least of your worries. Not like she's your mate or anything."

The words stung for reasons I couldn't explain, though I didn't deny the truth in them. Billie *wasn't* my mate, and if I was being honest, Tyler's death put things into quite the perspective for me. Whatever those lines were I was obsessing over before, they didn't matter. Raiden had told me that shifters only mated with their own kind, and Billie was a witch. Now, after everything, I felt like an idiot for making the lines such a priority. Why did I push so hard to force a mate bond between us when there was zero chance of it happening? *Didn't someone else tell you it was possible?* An image of purple hair filled my head and was gone in an instant, leaving me even more confused. I shook my head, running my fingers through my hair and sighed. "So what should I be worried about then? In your opinion."

"The pack, River. You should worry about your pack," Raiden answered. "They still don't have an alpha, and I've seen the way they look at you. You need to do what's right here."

"I'm in no condition to be anyone's alpha right now."

"Then change your condition. The wolves need you and you need them. Cut the shit and man up already."

I seriously regretted shifting back right about then. Raiden was right. Of course, he was right. If I hadn't been so concerned with protecting Billie in that quarry, Tyler might have stood a chance. I had spent so much time trying to keep her safe, I stopped caring about everyone else in my life. And whether or not I liked it, the pack was in my life now. Though I had to admit, I kind of liked it a lot.

Whatever I was going through, whatever Billie and I were going through, had to wait. The wolves were in trouble without an alpha to lead them and I had to listen to Raiden and step up. Maybe if I wasn't fighting what we all knew was coming from day one, things would have been different. There was only one reasonable choice. Do the right thing and hope it was enough to fill the void inside me.

With one glance toward the house looming in the distance, I straightened my back and pushed off the tree trunk. "Let's go see the wolves. I guess they got themselves an alpha."

Chapter
Thirty

Billie

"Nothing here either!" Vic yelled out over the pile of books she was tucked behind, tossing a hefty tome to the side. "Pass me the next one."

I reached for a leather-covered journal, but Logan beat me to the punch. The reaper slid one of the Shadowhurst history books Ms. Broussard brought from the town's archive library to Vic, and she jumped for it in excitement.

"Come on, baby," she murmured. "Give me what I'm looking for."

Vic flipped the pages, scanning the text with her fingertips as much as her eyes, and leaned against the wall. Her compact frame looked ridiculous amidst the wall of books she erupted, and I had to stop myself from laughing at my friend. At the opposite end of the Crystal Cauldron, Ms. Broussard busied herself with rearranging crystals on a shelf while we destroyed her small store with our presence. It amazed me how much the shop owner was willing to put up with. *She wasn't kidding before. She really is a friend to witches.*

My heart warmed at the thought. Friends were what I needed right now.

Turning my attention back to the Book of Darkness sprawled on my lap, I flipped the page to find a whole lot of nothing. We had been at this for hours, and so far, came up with nothing that got us closer to getting answers.

Stretching my neck, I trained a watchful eye at Logan. "Any luck on your end?"

"Bunch of rubbish," the reaper replied. "Nothing that could tell us who they might target next. The two I found that might have spirit element in their bloodlines are a lost cause. One's dead and the other is only part of the bloodline through marriage. Guess his wife was distantly related to someone from this shite town. And she's dead too, in case you're wondering."

I was wondering exactly that. Although now, I was basically trying not to throw up from hearing him throw the word 'dead' around.

As if he could sense my discomfort, Logan smiled sheepishly and slammed the book he was reading shut. "Sorry."

"It's okay," I lied. "Let's just concentrate on this and not worry about feelings right now."

"That I can do."

While Logan searched for another book to scour, I watched him. Every one of the reaper's moves was smooth and fluid like he was made entirely of water and air. I couldn't believe River was so concerned over this guy. So far, Logan had done nothing but help us in every way he could. Actually, come to think of it, he was helping me a hell of a lot more now than my own boyfriend was.

I scowled and tapped my finger on the thick binding of the grimoire.

"Do you miss it?" I blurted out before I could tell my dumb mouth to shut it.

Logan's lavender gaze pierced me from his corner of the shop. "Miss what?"

"Um..." I cleared my throat. "Home. England."

"Not at all," Logan answered. "Why?"

"Just wondering. You never talk about it." *What are you doing? Stop talking now, please.*

"Well, there are reasons for that. I didn't grow up in the best place. Things went down and I had to leave."

"Oh."

The shop had grown quiet, and I noticed Vic's eyes slant in our direction, eavesdropping no doubt.

"I tell you what," Logan said. "How about after we find Savannah and your other friends, I tell you all about the bloody hell I grew up in? For now, let's worry about one thing at a time."

I nodded and forced a smile. "Sounds good to me."

See, River? You were wrong. He's not hiding anything.

If I wasn't trying to give my boyfriend space to deal with things, I could have punched his teeth in. Or at least cover his stupid cute face in silver to make it sting a little. For some reason, imagining myself hurting River brought a sick joy to my heart and I shuddered at the thought. Guess I was more upset with him shutting me off than I realized.

I was still picturing all the ways I could make the stubborn boy squirm when Vic's bright voice filled the shop.

"Mother of the moon and stars," she yelped. "I think I got something!"

The two of us dropped what we were doing and crawled toward her, eyes bulging out of their sockets. Even Ms. Broussard put aside her crystals and meandered our way, towering over the three of us with the bell-shaped sleeves of her silk blouse brushing against my hair.

My palms spread as I strained my neck to see what Vic was pointing at. "What d'you find?"

"Possibly the place they might hold everyone," she announced proudly. "I can't believe it. It was under our noses the whole time!"

"What was?" Logan asked.

"The spell! The blood moon spell Catarina gave me from their collection."

I wasn't sure what she was getting at. Catarina had passed on the spell my mom stole for the rogue witches when she was playing secret agent, but it only encompassed how the High Coven was planning to open the portal. There was nothing in there that pointed to a location. At least not anything I noticed.

My brow creased. "You found a location in the spell?"

"Not exactly," Vic said. "But this part right here seemed odd to me when I read it. 'A power granted from below, its silence heavier than stone.' Get it?"

I did not.

By the looks of it, Logan and Ms. Broussard didn't either.

"Guys, come on!" Vic screeched, and I pressed an ear to my shoulder to muffle the sound. "The rogue witches thought this line pointed to the magic you could pull from the spell, the one that would open the portal. But it's not!"

"It's not?" I asked.

Victoria shook her head. "Not even close. It has nothing to do with magic. More the place itself. This instructs the witch performing the spell where she needs to do it. A place that has power that is more silent than stone."

"If I didn't feel dense before..." Logan muttered under

his breath, still as confused as the rest of us. "What place could be more silent than stone?"

"Library?" Vic asked and shrugged. "No, wait, that's not stone."

"Place of stone. Silent place of stone," I whispered. "Stone."

"Rain man," Vic said, nudging my arm. "What are you thinking?"

I took a deep breath and closed my eyes. The answer was so close, I could taste it on my tongue. Somehow, the wording made sense to me, as though I knew where this place was. My eyes snapped open, and my jaw slacked. "Goddess, that's it. A place more silent than stone. It's a graveyard, guys!"

Everyone fell silent and we took turns looking at each other in awe. I was right. It was the only thing that fit the description. A graveyard was as silent as it got and the stone in it was even more quiet. Tombstones didn't talk, neither did dead people. Pieces of ritual remnants danced before my eyes, and I whipped my head up to look at Ms. Broussard. "The witch cemetery in Carriage Hill, any chance they built it over something else?"

"Oh, dear," the shop owner said, her voice lowered. "It was so long ago, I'm uncertain. Why do you ask?"

I hissed out a breath. "When I went there with River, there were signs of ritual magic all over the place. Nothing recent, but the place had definitely been used for some spell-work a while back. The line Vic found mentioned a power granted from below. Maybe the cemetery was built over something. Something steeped in magic."

"More like steeped in death," Logan said, holding up his cellphone. "That place has old catacombs running under-neath it. Haven't been used in centuries, and when Carriage

Hill was founded, they covered them up, built the cemetery right over. At least according to my dear old friend *Wikipedia*."

That had to be it! The High Coven was using the catacombs to hide our friends while they collected everyone they needed. They must have shielded them with a spell I couldn't sense, which would explain why I wasn't able to find anything out of place. Not difficult to do considering how pathetic my magic had been lately.

I can't believe it!

Face regaining color, I tucked a loose strand of hair behind my ear and looked around the shop. "We got them!"

In front of me, Vic breathed out a chuckle. "So, what's the plan?"

"We get our friends back," I commanded. "And we show the High Coven that messing with any of us was a mistake."

Chapter Thirty-one

Billie

*L*ife had a ridiculous sense of humor. Either that, or it loved kicking my ass on regular intervals. Whatever it was, I wasn't loving my current situation one bit.

You'd think after figuring out the location the High Coven was keeping our friends, we'd go in all guns blazing. But no. That would be too easy. Instead, when I needed backup the most, no one was around.

River didn't answer his phone. Same with Peyton. And after what happened with Tyler, I had a feeling it would be a while until Abigail and Jayden rejoined the group.

At least Vic agreed to grab the rogue witches, leaving only myself and Logan trampling the pathway leading to the Carriage Hill cemetery like a couple of fools. What did we think we were going to do here? Take on the coven on our own?

Sure, on a good day, it may have been a good idea, but this wasn't a good day. I had zero control over my magic thanks to maybe-dad, and Logan, while good in a fight, couldn't exactly break a shielding spell.

As we got closer and the tombstones in the distance unfolded before us, I had only one thought. We were so freaking screwed.

Glancing back, I checked for Vic again and frowned.

"She'll be here," Logan reassured me, though I could hear the doubt in his voice. He was as worried as I was about our chances here.

"Let's hope so," I said. "We need the witches to drop the shield."

Logan's eyes narrowed. "Maybe not. Let's see if we can find another way into the catacombs. Dig our way down or something."

Dig our what where now? Is this guy for real?

I rolled my eyes and followed his lead despite every bone in my body wishing for the opposite. Even if Logan was right and we could get into the catacombs, nothing was stopping the High Coven from killing us on first sight. I doubted the coven left their precious cargo unprotected. For sure, there was at least one head witch guarding our friends. If not twenty.

Goddess help us.

Above our heads, birds flew in a perfect V and I shielded my eyes with my hand to watch them pass. They tore the sky so effortlessly, a sting of jealousy rushed through me. *Even the damn birds have backup.*

When we reached the hill River and I visited before, my chest buzzed with anxiety.

I stood to the side while Logan searched the cemetery for an entrance to the catacombs. Each time he shook his head, the pit in my stomach grew until I was so nauseous, I had to breathe harder just to keep from barfing. My fingers twitched and I continued to fight my body in a pathetic attempt to reach the magic I knew would stay dormant.

After my fourth failed try, I let out a frustrated sigh and leaned against the edge of a tombstone. My shoulders slumped and I spread my weight over the cool stone, muttering curses under my breath.

A loud caw sounded overhead, and I jumped back, startled. My butt hit the tombstone, wiggling the deteriorating thing out of the earth and tilting it backward. With my balance out the window, I toppled back, shrieking as my feet bounced off each other to send me flying in the air.

When my shoulder hit the hard earth, I should have been relieved. Except I wasn't. Because now, I was rolling. There must have been a ditch behind the plot I didn't see, and my stupid clumsy body fell right into it. Rocks scraped my cheeks and twigs caught in my hair while I rolled into oblivion, screaming the entire time.

When I finally stopped, I was so beaten up, I was surprised I could feel my arms and legs at all.

Brushing dirt off my clothes, I dug out the leaves and branches now living in my hair and struggled to right myself. My gaze trailed up the ditch I fell into, and nausea returned in tenfold. On the horizon, Logan's head popped up into view.

"Sleeping on the job, I see," he teased.

A deep growl rocked my chest. "Stop joking around and come help me get out of here. I think I broke my butt."

Logan's laughter echoed all the way down as he descended to meet me, and I fought the urge to knock him out cold. Extending a hand, he helped to my feet, but his eyes drifted past my shoulder.

I whipped around, shock spreading down my body in tidal waves. "Is that?"

Logan grinned. "I think so."

We exchanged looks before taking off into a dead sprint toward the rusted manhole cover a few feet away from us. Grass gathered around it in clumps, and I noticed the places it had been cut away to allow the lid to open.

"This was used," I announced. "Recently."

Without a word, Logan reached for the brown-colored handle and pulled. The scraping sound of metal on metal rose over us, and my thighs clenched up in response. As Logan dragged the manhole cover aside, I cringed. Taking a step in, we looked into the hole and exhaled in unison.

"Guess this is it, mate," Logan said, a shiver in his voice. "Ready?"

I pulled out my cellphone, seeing no response from any of our friends or River. Brushing my hair back, I tucked the phone into my back pocket and gave the cemetery one last look around. The silence that greeted me was an answer in itself.

Glancing from Logan to the metal ladder leading down into what I was certain would be our doom, I straightened my back and filled my lungs with air. "Let's get it over with."

Then we started to climb.

Chapter
Thirty-two

River

The pack kept their eyes on me the entire time I shifted into human form, and their staring made me that much more uncomfortable. I was pretty used to shifting by now, but coming back to my body wasn't exactly the same as becoming the wolf. For starters, it ended with all my bits hanging out. Not an experience that required an audience as far as I was concerned. Whoever made up the idiotic rule that an alpha shifts last deserved to get beaten into a pulp. What an atrocity.

As soon as I could stand, I turned away from the pack and reached for the spare clothes I left in the clearing behind the resistance house. The others followed suit, dressing only after I had. Another dumb rule, I wagered.

When we were all decent, I gambled to turn around, relieved not to be met with a wave of exposed skin.

"Good run!" Griffin exclaimed, patting me on the back. Then lowering his voice only for me to hear, "I think even Isaac liked that one."

I followed his gaze to the man that used to lead the pack

that was now mine and forced a friendly smile to my face. My smile was returned with a twitching upper lip and a low growl. Guess some things never changed. Isaac was still an asshole.

Not paying him any mind, I made my way to the rest of the pack, handing out bottles of water from the crate we stored at a nearby tree. Each person thanked me, backing away when I came too close as a sign of respect. I wasn't sure how I felt about all of this. The pack acted like I was some self-crowned king, and the idea irritated me to no small extent. It was one thing to offer leadership and guidance to these people, and quite another to be feared. I didn't want my pack afraid of me. What I wanted was their friendship and support.

We'll have to work on that, don't we? I asked my wolf. His whimpers vibrated in my chest, letting me know he agreed. *And soon.*

When I handed out the last of the water, I let the group chat amongst themselves and scurried into the shadows of the trees. Luckily, they were too busy with the excitement of our run to notice me disappear, giving me a chance to get my head straight.

Lowering to sit on a fallen tree trunk, I reached for my cellphone. My finger hovered over the notification bubble and my chest tightened.

Seven missed calls from Billie.

My head swam while I tried to work up the nerve to call her back. In the last few days, things with the pack had been so easy, I didn't want to let go. But this wasn't fair to Billie, and I hated being such a tremendous asshole. Eventually, we would have to discuss what happened with Tyler and it was best to rip the bandaid off and hope not to bleed out.

"Just call her already," a shrill voice sounded behind me.

I twisted around to see Peyton emerge from the trees. The soul sucker strolled toward me with newfound confidence, and I shrank in my seat. *Since when did Peyton Ling get to be so damn scary?*

She crouched beside me, eyes darting to the phone. "You know she'll be pissed if you keep this up."

"I know," I whispered. "I'm going to call. I just needed some space."

"Big bad alpha needed a cuddle from the group?" Peyton teased.

I chuckled. "Something like that. So, what have you been up to?"

Darkness floated behind Peyton's eyes, making me uneasy. It was gone before I could mention it, leaving a nasty taste in mouth. Something was bothering Peyton, and as much as I wanted to talk to her about it, I doubted I'd make her feel any better. Talking Peyton down from the ledge was always Billie's specialty. *One more reason to stop avoiding her.*

"This town is seriously fucked," Peyton finally said.

Smiling, I coughed out a laugh and buried my feet into the ground. "Something is always wrong, isn't it? We can never get a break."

More shadows danced in her eyes, and I wondered what it was Peyton didn't want to tell me. We weren't close friends, not by any means, but I had hoped after everything our group had been through, she'd trust me enough with at least some of her issues.

When she kept quiet, I nudged her side. "Come on, what's on your mind?" I urged. "I know I'm not Billie, but lay it on me."

Peyton laughed.

I just stared like an idiot.

"I've been thinking about all those girls Billie said we can't remember. Trying to wrap my head around it. I don't get it. I mean, like I want to believe her, and I do, really, but..."

"It sounds batshit crazy."

The soul sucker frowned. "To the max."

"Weirder shit has happened," I suggested. "I'm willing to bet this isn't even the worst this town has to offer. You know, sometimes, I wish I never found about witches and shadowers and the rest of this crap. No offense."

"None taken. And me too. But then, if you didn't..."

Peyton wiggled her eyebrows, and I shook my head. "No Billie and me. I know. Not a trade-off I'm willing to take. And who knows, maybe if we're not chasing our tails here, we get these girls back and everything goes back to normal."

"Speak for yourself, wolf boy. I'm not chasing tail anytime soon."

A laugh escaped me, and I found it jarring to know it wasn't forced. Beside me, Peyton smiled and rolled back on her heels until she was sitting on the ground, her legs outstretched in front of her. The red streaks of her hair played in the wind, and I noticed her body relax for the first time in days. Whatever was happening in Shadowhurst may have gotten us all messed up, but I knew we were better than this. Better than giving up. That it took me this long to get around to it made me feel like a complete loser and I pressed the home screen button of my phone, scrolling to Billie's name in the call log.

I was about to dial her number when another name

flashed on the screen. An inbound call. Bringing the phone up to my ear, I closed my eyes and breathed out. "Vic?"

Next to me, Peyton's eyebrows raised in interest.

"Are you serious?" I asked the witch. "Okay, meet us there. We'll be there soon. Oh, and Vic?" I added. "Hurry UP."

When I clicked off the call, the taste of acid and fear coated the roofs of my mouth. My body heated, and deep down, the wolf howled in a restless panic. Pocketing the phone, I rose to stand, looking down at Peyton. "We need to go. They found out where the High Coven is keeping the girls. Billie went there with Logan, but Vic can't get a hold of her. She thinks something happened."

Peyton jumped up faster than a rocket.

"Get whoever you can from the house, I'll meet you up front," she said. "I'm sure she's fine. Let's go."

You better be fine, babe. You better be fine enough to kick my ass for being such a prick lately.

Chapter
Thirty-three

Billie

The catacombs buried deep under the witch cemetery were pretty much as revolting as you would assume. Nope, that's not true. They were worse.

The corridors Logan and I walked through carried us deep into the abyss of the underground, and each winding step inward sent a coldness through my bones I couldn't describe with enough words. If I had to try, I would say this was terror in its most fertile state. Logan stayed close to my side, and I could sense his trepidation each time a creaking noise boomed around us. Which happened on more occasions than I liked. Lighting the ghostly darkness with our phones, we marched onward, storing our fears as deeply as we could while searching for any sign of our friends.

Despite the gnawing doom threatening to overcome me, it relieved me to have Logan here. At least I wasn't alone in this nightmare.

A loud scrape sounded behind us, and we both turned in unison, blood draining from our faces.

"What was that?" Logan asked, shielding me with his arm.

I searched the empty passageway and grimaced. "Not sure. Let's keep moving."

We spun around, facing forward once more. Or what I assumed was forward. It was impossible to tell right from left down here, and we had gotten turned around so many times, I couldn't even recall the direction we came from. Wherever it was didn't matter. We had to find our friends, then worry about the way out.

My fingers felt the cold wall lining our side and I let the history of this place rush through me. It was dreadful. Absolutely freaking mortifying.

Never in my life did I imagine that I'd be sneaking my way through the place that once housed so many dead. *And I thought Shadowhurst was bad.* Compared to this, the town was looking like a damn wonderland.

Another scrape pierced the air, this one closer than the first.

"Seriously, mate," Logan said. "I think someone's following us."

We turned again, throwing up our hands to light the corridor outstretching behind us, and this time, our phones were not the only beacons in the murky space. My lashes fluttered as several orbs of light floated toward us, bouncing with the steps of whoever was carrying them. Heart bobbing in my throat, I widened my stance, reaching for the knife tucked in the secret compartment of my boot. I clutched the hilt and glanced at Logan, then narrowed my eyes at the approaching intruders.

The bright lights obscured my view and for once, I knew

exactly how a deer felt when a car flashed its high beams in its beady eyes.

Lowering my cellphone, I tilted my head to the side. "River?"

"Hey, babe," my boyfriend said, cutting the silence.

I stared at him with an open mouth. "What are you doing here? Is that Peyton?"

"Hey, B!" My best friend popped her head out from behind River's wide shoulders. "This place is hella freaky, huh?"

"Um, yeah. What are you guys doing here? I couldn't get a hold of anyone. How did you know where to find us?"

River's eyebrows scrunched and he moved closer to stand in front of me. "Vic called, told us where you two were."

I glanced past him to see no one else around. "Where is she? Are the rogue witches coming?"

"They are," River said. "They'll be here soon, but we wanted to catch you before you got any further."

Well, this sounds ominous.

I brushed my hair back, urging River to spill the beans with a shrug.

"The rogue witches found something and you won't like it."

What the hell now? "What is it? Is Vic okay?"

"She's fine," River whispered. "But you might want to sit down for this."

My thoughts jumbled into a thick mess, and I struggled to regain control of my mouth. There were so many words rushing through me, I couldn't pick out one clear sentence to hold on to. Though, *screw this* made an appearance on over one occasion. I had to admit, it was the best way to describe how I felt after River told me what the rogue witches unearthed.

"Babe?" River asked, lightly shaking my shoulder. "You good?"

"Um, I guess. Just trying to wrap my head around all this," I answered. "You're sure that's what she said? No chance you heard wrong?"

He shook his head 'no' and my soul died a little.

"So, let me get this straight. Graves tried to steal all five fae powers and that's why Evanora's spell was in the Book of Darkness?"

Peyton frowned. "That's what Vic said. I guess your ancestor wasn't happy with whatever magic the fae dolled out, so she wrote the spell. Evanora must have found it and decided to do the same. It's messed up."

"But Graves didn't succeed?"

"Not as far as the rogue witches told Vic. She got four of the elements, but the fae stopped her before she sucked up spirit powers," River answered. "Which is weird. Doesn't she already have spirit powers? I mean, that's how you got them, right?"

My head throbbed at the temples, and I rubbed them to ease the pain. "I have no clue," I breathed out. "No one knows anything about the fae, not really. Maybe whatever spirit magic she had wasn't strong enough. At least not as strong as magic taken directly from the source. I seriously don't know anymore."

"Good enough guess as any." Peyton shrugged. "So you're like what? A super witch now?"

"I wouldn't say that. I'm able to control the earth, air, and water elements," I said in a hushed tone. "Because of whatever Graves did. She had the elements in her blood after she performed the spell and passed them down to all the women in her lineage. And if my assumption is true, I only have a sliver of whatever power the spirit element has. But I can't control fire. Why?"

"Maybe you can and don't know it?" Logan suggested.

I ignored the annoyed look River shot his way.

"I guess," I mused. "Back in the resistance house when the shifters fought, I almost had it though. Maybe I haven't tapped into it yet because of the block on my magic."

"Yeah, about that," River said. "You sure this shadow asshole is the one that blocked your magic?"

I told them everything right after River filled me in on what Vic discovered. No matter how badly I wanted to keep the messed up situation with maybe-dad to myself, there couldn't be any more secrets between us. The shadow man said he would return my powers when I was ready, whatever the hell that meant, and I couldn't continue to battle this on my own. River and our friends deserved to know the truth in case something went wrong, and I couldn't get my magic back. They deserved to be prepared for the worst possible scenario. I had no choice but to tell them. No matter how crazy it made me look.

I rolled my neck, rubbing the tension gathering at its base with my clammy fingers. "I'm sure," I said. "That guy did something to me to keep my magic blocked, which would explain why I can't tap into the fire element. If what Vic said is true, I should have all four elements in my blood thanks to Graves." A thought tugged at my brain. "Wait, you think my mom has them too?"

River and Logan kissed their teeth in unison.

"I mean, probably," Peyton said. "It would make sense since it's her lineage and whatever. She never mentioned it?"

"No. But it's not like we were besties." I frowned. "Something is bothering me about all of this," I said. "Graves performed this idiotic spell and now, I can control earth, air, water, and maybe fire. What about the spirit fae powers I have?"

"Well, we know the original witches got frisky with the fae," Peyton suggested. "That's probably it."

"That doesn't make sense," I said. "If it was Graves, she would have had all five fae elements in her magic, and according to Vic and the rogue witches, she only succeeded in summoning four. I doubt the fae would have risked passing off spirit powers to her after what she did, and she was the only original witch my family is linked to. It just doesn't add up. I got fae powers somehow, and it wasn't from Graves."

From the looks on everyone's faces, I could tell they agreed with me. A piece was missing, and no matter how hard I tried, I couldn't put it together. Somehow, I ended up with all the fae powers and it was driving me crazy not to know how. Unless...

"NO!" I screeched, making everyone around me jump. "What if he's not lying?"

"Who?" River asked.

Fists tightened in my lap. "The shadow man. What if he really is my father? What if he's a spirit fae?"

"Girl, that's pretty far fetched, no?" Peyton asked. "You said it yourself. The fae haven't shown their faces in ages."

"And Daria, that dumb fox, said they're coming for me. I think it's safe to assume we know nothing at all."

Near to me, Logan sighed. "Well, we know that

Savannah is in these catacombs right now and she needs our help. How about we get her and the other girls out of this bloody place then worry about your sordid family?"

River cursed under his breath and Peyton rolled her eyes while I struggled to stand. My chest grew heavy, and tears threatened to pool behind my lids. I wanted to brush this aside and keep moving, but I couldn't do it. Graves made a colossal mistake messing with fae powers, and because of her, our entire family line was screwed. I was an abomination. A witch with powers she should never have, and I hated myself for it. I didn't want this magic, and for the first time, I was glad I couldn't tap into any of it. My own ancestor went against everything witches valued. She stole powers that weren't hers. Took energy that didn't belong to her. It was repulsive.

Nothing good could come out of this.

Nothing at all.

Blinking, I stopped trying to keep myself together. Hot tears fell down my face as I thought about the monster I was, and choking gasps flew from my lips.

I leaned against the icy wall of the catacombs and closed my eyes. My lungs constricted and wheezed as I gulped air that did little to ease the tension in my heart. Sweat beaded down my back. Voices carried over me in jumbled echoes.

Tightening my fists, I punched the wall and let out a broken cry.

I fell apart.

Chapter Thirty-four

River

*B*illie's cries filled the catacombs while I stood dumbfounded at her side. I wasn't sure what scared me more, her breakdown, or the fact that if her cries got any louder, someone would hear us. Her tears dripped down her face and her hair clung to her forehead in sweaty clumps as she repeated the same words over and over again. *Abomination. Monster. Freak.*

My heart shattered into pieces and the wolf howled under my skin.

"Babe," I whispered, putting a hand on her back and rubbing circles over her shaking body. "Babe, please, breathe. You're fine. Everything is fine."

"Nothing is fine!" she hissed, landing another fist to the wall. The stone shook under her blows, crumbling in small pieces to the ground.

If I couldn't calm her down, she was going to break her damn hands.

Taking a deep breath in, I wrapped my arms around her stomach and pulled her into me. Her body shook against my chest and a low growl vibrated in me in response. The wolf wanted to protect her, but he didn't know how. Something we currently had in common.

I pressed my lips to her neck, breathing heated air onto her skin. "Billie, please. Try to calm down. Talk to me."

"I'm a freak," she choked out. "Everything about me is wrong. I don't want this magic. I don't want any magic at all."

Next to us, Peyton and Logan shifted uncomfortably in their spots. Their mouths opened and closed as they tried to think of something to say but no one spoke. I couldn't blame them. What the hell could any of us say right now? We had no clue what she was going through.

"You're not a freak," I whispered into her neck. "This isn't your fault."

"It's my family's fault. They made me this way. Graves didn't think of anyone but herself, and now, I have to pay the price. Why didn't my mom tell me about this? Why didn't she warn me?"

I didn't know what to say.

Pressing my lips into a tight line, I spun her around to face me. "Moms don't always get it right," I said. "Mine sure as shit didn't. Beatrix was probably trying to protect you from this, and judging by what I'm seeing now, I kind of have to agree."

Billie's brow creased and she tensed in my embrace. "You're kidding me, right? What the actual hell, River?!?"

I resisted the urge to laugh. Even in her most troubled time, Billie still found it in herself to tell me off. *That's my girl!*

"Hear me out here," I said, raising both my hands up in surrender. "I know you think having these powers is wrong—"

"It's not just wrong," she interrupted. "It goes against everything witches stand for. We don't steal magic. There is a balance that must be upheld, and for Graves to do this was atrocious. She took power that didn't belong to her, from people that gifted her magic in the first place, and she passed it on to every witch born into her lineage. It's sickening."

"Or is it kind of amazing?"

"No."

"Maybe it's actually a good thing?"

"Also no."

Yeah, this isn't going so well.

Glancing at Peyton and Logan, I took a step back from Billie to give her some space. Crowding her wasn't working and she was getting more worked up the more I pressed her. I had to try a fresh approach.

"Here's the thing, witch," I chided. "Since when does Billie Stonewall freak out over having unknown magic?"

"One more word, hunter, and I'll end you."

Now we're getting somewhere. "With what?" I asked. "You don't want your magic, right? So, what can you do about it? How about the three of us go get the girls and you can stay here and wait until we're back? That way you can keep yourself from having to use the powers you don't even want."

Near us, Peyton's eyebrows shot up and she muttered something under her breath. Swearing, no doubt. I didn't let it bother me. I was getting somewhere here, and no one knew Billie as I did. There was only one way to get her out of this slump, and I knew my girl well enough to know that coddling her would not do it. Billie needed to feel in control, and I was going to give her control in spades.

"So, do we have a deal, witch?" I asked. "We go save our friends and you stay here."

"NOT. HAPPENING."

I chuckled. "That's what I thought."

"I hate you," Billie hissed.

Another chuckle escaped me. "Yeah, I don't think that's true."

To my surprise, her lips curled up and she greeted me with a half-smile. *Welcome back, my crazy girl.*

"My family is seriously messed up," Billie said, and I let my shoulders relax.

"Whose isn't?" I joked. "At least yours gave you some kickass magic. My mom only made sure I had a tail. Wanna trade?"

She laughed and my heart beat faster.

"I know this is a lot to find out," I added. "And you have every right to hate what happened in your family's past, but there's a whole other angle you're not seeing here."

"And what's that?"

Brushing a lock of hair behind her ear, I found her eyes and held her gaze. "That this magic you have doesn't have to be a bad thing. Sure, it may not have come to be in the best way, but this is good."

Billie's face dropped.

"How can something be good if it came from such evil intentions?"

I smiled. "Because the witch who has these powers now isn't evil. You're good, Billie. The kindest, most selfless person I know. What you do with this magic is your choice, but I know that whatever you choose, it will be because it's the right thing to do. Don't hate your magic for finding you in the shitty way it did. Embrace it for what you can do with it.

Use it to help us free our friends. Use it for something noble."

The darkness gathering in Billie's eyes subsided and she blew out a long breath. Her shoulders slumped as she leaned against the wall, uncurling the fists she'd been holding.

"I'm still pissed at you for going awol," she announced, making me grin. "Not cool, hunter."

"I know and I'm sorry. I got caught up in my own stuff and it was wrong. But I'm here now, and I hope you forgive me. I'm never leaving you to deal with any of this stuff alone. I promise."

Billie shook her head, and I could see the steam in her dwindle. I meant what I said. It was unfair of me to push her away. Teaches me right for listening to Raiden when I should have been listening to my heart all along. My eyes sparkled and I found Billie's gaze again in the dim-lit corridor. "Oh, there's some news I have for you."

"Oh, Goddess, no!" she cried out. "Not anything else bad, please!"

I shook my hand. "Nothing bad, I swear. I may have kind of sort of taken on the alpha role with the pack."

"Wait, what?" Billie and Logan asked in unison.

"Girl," Peyton snapped from behind us. "Your boyfriend like totally schooled those wolves. Which reminds me, I should probably go get them."

"They're here?" Billie asked.

"Yep," I said. "I asked for their help, and they didn't even bat an eye. Pretty cool, huh? Peyton and I figured we could use all the help we could get here."

"You figured right."

The musty air stilled around us, and I watched as Billie's face scrunched while her brain worked out the details. The tears that streamed down her face had all but dried, leaving behind only remnants of mascara. With the black streaks across her cheeks and her eyes twinkling in the light of our cellphones, she looked like a damn warrior, and I loved it. Magic or not, my girl was a force to be reckoned with and she was back now. I could see it in the way she moved. This was the same fearless girl I fell in love with and despite what life had thrown at her, I knew she'd find her way to us.

Billie was ready.

We had to be too.

Running my thumb across her cheek, I wiped off the dark stains. "So, what do you want to do?"

"Get our friends," she announced. "I want to get our friends and I want to get the hell out of here. Get your pack, alpha. We're going in!"

As her words rushed through the catacombs, another sound pierced the air and this one made the hairs on my arms stand on edge. The four of us exchanged glances, swallowing hard as a bloodcurdling scream tore through the corridor from deep inside the catacombs.

I didn't need to check with the others to know who it belonged to.

Savannah was hurt, badly hurt, and we had no more time left to waste.

Chapter Thirty-five

Billie

"Peyton, watch out!" I yelled as a massive rock burst from the wall of the catacombs and flew toward my best friend.

She ducked down, the rock missing her by only a few inches.

Relief flooded me when Peyton looked my way and flashed two thumbs up. She jumped to her feet in seconds, twisting around to stand between two enormous wolves, one brown and one white as snow.

All around us, magic bounced off the walls as the head witches fought to push us away. Howls cut the air each time a wolf got hit, and I had to turn my head right and left to make sure it wasn't River.

I didn't know what we were expecting to find when we followed Savannah's screams through the catacombs, but this sure wasn't it.

When we burst into the large opening Savannah's voice carried us to, my jaw hit the ground. The High Coven didn't just plant a few head witches to hold down our friends. They brought the whole damn cavalry.

I should have been afraid when we saw them, petrified, really, but I felt only one thing. Happiness. I was ecstatic to see all my friends again.

In the center of what looked to be a large burial site, Savannah, Lorelei, Mel, and Morgan lay chained to the floor. Their arms and legs outstretched to the side, held down by heavy metal rings that bound them to the ground. Around them, a salt circle spread out, connecting their bodies. In its center, an empty slot remained.

The last piece of the spell. The last person to complete it.

On either side of our friends, small openings carved into the stone walls. They were large enough to fit human remains, and my stomach turned when I noticed the bones lining each one. This was where they placed the bodies when the catacombs were still in use.

This place seriously sucks.

In the circle, Savannah screamed again, and I spun my head to watch a head witch slice her arm open. Dark red blood poured down her wrist and into the ground beneath her, flowing in a line to inch closer to Morgan's wrist. Horror washed over me as I watched the same head witch walk to Morgan, about to slice her open just the same.

My blood boiled at the sight, and I pumped my legs to get closer to stop her only to be shoved back by invisible winds. To my right, another blast pushed against River while he fought to reach me. My eyes darted to the circle, seeing four head witches move in to block us. Their arms stretched out, working the winds with pulsing amethysts in their hands. Behind them, Sebyl, Theodora, Luna, and Rhiamon clutched hands and chanted words in a language I didn't understand. Sebyl's eyes were shut so tight, I could make out every wrinkle on her face. Next to her, Theodora's massive beehive of hair brushed the low ceiling as she swayed from side to side. Rhiamon and Luna stared blankly ahead, not at me and not at the circle. Their eyes unfocused and their lips parted, making them look like broken wind-up dolls. The priestesses had been in this state since we first barged in on the sickening display, not once acknowledging our presence.

They don't think I'm a threat.

As well they shouldn't have. I wasn't a threat, not in the slightest. Even though River talked me off the ledge and insisted my magic was not as bad as I thought—which I still wasn't entirely convinced of—I could feel no power inside me to pull from. Not that it shocked me. I didn't expect my magic to appear as soon as I made my peace with it. This wasn't a fairytale, it was my life. And right about now, my life sucked big.

Peeling my gaze off the high priestesses, I looked to River, mouthing words I hoped he could understand.

"Break the circle," I whispered. "Break the circle."

He nodded and relief overloaded my system. Crab-walking backward, he struggled against the currents that pushed on us to inch closer to his pack.

The wolves howled and whined, jumping to avoid the magic the head witches threw at them. There were so many witches in the damn place, I lost count at twenty.

Like I said, they brought the freaking cavalry. And what did we bring?

My eyes wetted as they struck another wolf with a huge fireball and Logan jumped to put the fires out.

A whole lot of nothing useful was what we brought. *DAMN IT ALL TO HELL.*

With the wind whipping my skin, I swerved out of its way with a grunt. Pushing my body up, I dodged hit after hit, scrambling to get to a spot where I could be out of reach from the witches attacking me. Someone screamed and the witches jumped to follow the sound, giving me a chance to bolt. Holding back vomit, I crawled into an open slot in the wall, plugging my nose to keep the rancid smell from penetrating my system. It didn't work. Obviously.

The disgusting aroma of old bones scurried up my nose and I swallowed the nausea coating my mouth. Careful not to crush the bones beneath me, I closed my eyes and placed my hands on the stone.

Come on magic. Give me what you got!

It didn't.

Instead, all I felt was the rumble of the catacombs as a head witch blasted two wolves with a lightning bolt large enough to take down a tree.

A gasp broke free and I tumbled back, causing something to crack beneath my weight.

Please, don't be a skull. Please don't be a skull.

I looked down. *Well, shit.*

Shaking disturbing thoughts from my head, I forced my hands to the stone again and searched for my magic. It met me with another bout of emptiness.

About to give up, I started to climb out of the grave I crawled into when something caught my eyes.

"No freaking way!" I shrieked, jumping down to inch closer.

Near to me, shadows crept over the walls. Their fingers inched across the stone, gathering into a massive form that resembled a creepy-ass cloud. My heart raced and I looked down at my hands, wondering if this was my doing. I frowned.

My palms were free of shadow magic.

If it isn't me, who is it? I wondered a second too late.

Before I could put the pieces together, a horrid scream blasted through the catacombs, making me drop to my knees.

"LOGAN!"

By the time Peyton's voice reached me, Logan's body was already being pulled into the circle. Old, decrepit tree roots wrapped around his legs, dragging him into the hell that awaited. In the circle, flanked by more head witches than I could count, Sebyl smiled. Her thin lips spread wider, and her nose sharpened to a point. The priestess' eyes flashed to me before landing back on Logan. She twirled her fingers and the roots tightened over him, yanking him into the center of the circle.

Straight into the empty slot reserved for the spirit element.

"No, that can't be right," I whispered to no one in particular.

But I knew I was wrong to think it. It was very freaking right. Logan was the missing link. Born with spirit fae blood under a blood moon.

Sebyl's magic wrapped the roots around his arms and legs, securing him in place. Her eyes shut again and a head witch moved toward Logan to slit his wrists as she had done with all the others. The high priestesses continued their chants. The spell continued to take shape.

All I could do was watch as it all unfolded. Watch the priestesses bring the spell to life, and Logan's shadow magic disperse around him as his blood drained into the circle.

Logan had fae magic like me, and he was going to be our undoing.

Chapter
Thirty-six

Billie

*L*ogan's face contorted as the blood continued to pour from his open wound and into the circle. His eyes met mine and he shakily nudged his head in Savannah's direction. His lips moved, but I couldn't make out anything over the screams filling the catacombs. Logan gritted his teeth, mouthing words again, and my heart broke when I finally understood. "Save her first."

The high priestesses chanted faster and faster until every word melted into the next. The circle my friends fed with their blood glowed a bright blue, and a sickening dread filled my bones. It was the same blue as the portal we saw not long ago.

"Crap!" I yelled. Then turning to River and Peyton, I screamed, "They almost have it. We need to do something, and fast!"

River nodded and dropped to his knees. His bones snapped and his back curled as he reformed, leaving his human body. In seconds, a massive gray wolf stood in River's place. The wolf howled and ten others jogged to his side.

Their teeth bared and warm saliva spilled from their jaws as they stomped their paws into the ground. Behind them, more wolves gathered, all ready to attack.

"Distract the head witches," I commanded. "Peyton and I will try to break the circle."

The wolves did as I asked, with River leading the way as they charged for the witches. Furry, muscled bodies clashed with bouts of magic, and shouts filled the space we crowded.

I didn't stay to watch, even though seeing River in his element was the most breathtaking thing I've ever encountered. Seemed Peyton felt the same since I had to all but drag her away. "Eyes on the prize!" I hissed, tugging her after me. "You can ogle the pack later."

She chuckled and followed me to the furthest wall of the catacombs. Our backs pressed against the stone, inching closer to the circle and staying in the shadows as best we could. It was an impossible task considering the light the circle was casting, but worth a shot nonetheless.

We were almost at Savannah's feet when a head witch snapped her neck toward us, a snarl on her face.

The witch shot her hands out, and I only had enough time to shove Peyton out of the way as a brilliant bolt of lightning flew toward us. It hit my shoulder, twisting me around and pushing me into the wall. My forehead smashed on the stone, a blinding pain bursting behind my eyes. My head throbbed and my vision blurred as I worked to keep standing. Knees weak, I checked to make sure Peyton wasn't injured, and when I saw her jump for Savannah again, a scream burst from my lips.

"Watch out!" I shouted.

Peyton darted her eyes and twirled on her tiptoes to

avoid another hit. The lightning tore past her, colliding with the wall in sparks.

Shielding my eyes, I shook off the numbing pain in my shoulder and ran toward my friend. The witch flaunted her magic, showing me her hands before she thrust another bolt in my direction.

This one would not miss.

It barreled toward me at a speed so high, I had no time to avoid it. My eyes bulged and my neck froze as I watched the lightning rush straight for my chest.

Suddenly, a large stone flew past me, colliding with the lightning bolt only seconds before it did me in. I gulped, turning my head to the right and breathed out a delirious laugh.

There, at the furthest entrance to the catacombs, Vic stood surrounded by rogue witches. Her eyes narrowed and her fingers spread wide as she worked the crystals in her grasp to fire at the witch before me. Wind caught the woman by the legs, knocking her on her ass.

The witch shrieked.

Vic laughed.

It was freaking amazing.

While I continued to crawl to Savannah with Peyton on my heels, Vic and the rogue witches split up. Catarina commanded one group to help River and the pack, while Vic worked with the rest, attacking the head witches from behind. *They're fencing them in!*

Relief overtook me and I exchanged a knowing glance with Peyton. Without speaking, we dove for the circle with me running to Savannah while Peyton rushed for Morgan. Landing on my knees at Savannah's side, I lifted her limp head and tested for a pulse. She lost so much blood, was still losing it, but she was alive. I grasped the metal rings binding her to the ground, pulling on them with all my might.

They didn't budge.

"This isn't working! Any luck on your end?" I asked Peyton in a panic.

"They're in too deep," she responded.

My head snapped to the outer edge of the circle, which was glowing even brighter now. Sebyl and the other priest-esses did not stop their chanting. It was almost as though they knew we stood no chance at freeing our friends.

The blue of the circle intensified, and ripples formed in the surrounding air. *Oh, shit. Is it working? Is this it?* I looked around, searching for a sign that a portal was opening. For this other world, the coven was trying to access.

But I saw nothing.

One look at Sebyl told me she had the same realization.

"Peyton! I don't think it's working!" I yelled out. "Something is wrong!"

"Good!" Peyton shouted back. "Means we have more time."

We tore at the bindings holding our friends simultaneously. Sweat beaded down my forehead and my heart pounded fast enough to hurt. Wrapping my icy fingers around the ring, I buried a boot into the ground and pulled. The ring strained, but I could feel it give way. "I almost have—"

A blast of magic collided with my back and sent me flying forward. Pain unlike any other tore at my skin and I could feel every bone in my body give up. Knees hitting the ground first, I choked on spit as the rest of my body followed. My chest hit something hard, and when I opened the eyes I've been clenching shut, I saw that I landed on top of Logan.

His eyes widened and he groaned from the weight of me. "I'm pretty sure your boyfriend won't like this, love," he teased. I noticed drops of blood at the edge of his lips.

"Just shut up," I hissed, forcing myself to stand up. As I moved, sharp pains spread down my back and I stumbled forward, falling on Logan again. "Shit! Someone got me good."

I tried again, this time moving slower and scrambling to my knees. My back felt like someone shredded all the skin and I refused to look for fear I might vomit from what I saw. Instead, I reached for the roots binding Logan to the floor and pulled. When they didn't budge, I sliced at them with my knife.

Slice after slice, I worked to free him, while Logan thrashed on the ground beneath me. Magic flashed above our heads, and screams and howls covered the catacombs in a blanket of chaos. No matter how much I cut, the roots didn't budge.

I fell to my hands, punching the ground with a loud groan. "UGH! It isn't working!"

Logan whispered something I couldn't understand. My eyes met his and I realized all too late that he was fading. The light in his eyes disappeared and his head lolled to the side like a stringless puppet. I gasped, pressing my hands to his chest.

"NO! Don't you dare pass out on me right now!"

Digging my nails into Logan's shirt, I shook him hoping to keep his eyes open, but he only slunk further down in my grasp. Jaw clenched, my eyes threatened to pool, and I fought against the tears. *This is no time to cry. FIX him!*

While I searched for something to cut Logan free, the high priestesses continued to attempt the portal spell. The only solace I had at the moment was their pathetic failure, and it made a small smile break the tight seal of my lips. I moved to check Logan's pulse when something warmed inside my jean pocket. Digging in, I pulled out the staurolite and brought it up to my face. It seemed the same as always with one small difference. It was blistering hot to the touch.

I yelped, dropping the stone to the ground and shaking my hand to ease the burn. My entire body set ablaze and I curled over Logan's unconscious body, my head hanging in my chest. Teeth chattering, I worked against the scream building up deep inside of me.

Every blood cell pulsed under my skin and my vision swam before me. My lungs expanded and I blew out the breath I've been holding, freezing in my spot. Instead of a gasp or a scream, a wild wind exploded from my lips and knocked Theodora backward. She caught my eyes, tripping to get back into position with her coven sisters. Before she could, my hands shot out to the side, one summoning fire while the other dripped wet with water.

I pushed them both in her direction and stared wide-eyed as my elemental magic shoved her away from the other high priestesses.

When Theodora hit the wall with a thud, all their eyes snapped to me. I raised my hands above me, reaching for the rock over our heads, and pulled the stone down one by one. It fell in rapid-fire, tumbling at the women's feet and making them scurry away from the circle. Away from my friends.

Sebyl's gaze found me at the same time as a bone-charring flame spread through my chest and I buckled backward. Tearing at my sweater, I rubbed the skin, checking for a wound.

"Mother of fae," I whispered, still glaring at my chest like an idiot.

My eyes blinked as though I hooked them up to a battery and my shoulders tensed. Black lines spread across my chest and up my neck. Their swirling patterns pulsed, and they reflected light so brilliantly, it looked like the Aurora Borealis had found a new home on my body.

"Well, this is different," I choked out. My fingers trailed the pattern of the lines, desperately wanting to keep staring as they expanded over every inch of my body.

But this was not the time for that. Closing my eyes, I reached for my shadows and let out a relieved laugh when they rushed to the surface with no objection at all. I had my magic back. I had all of it. And it felt too damn good to do nothing with.

Grinning, I snapped my head up and looked for River.

Chapter
Thirty-seven

River

*G*riffin's wolf body-checked me out of the way and we tumbled sideways just as a growing fireball rushed by us. I tripped over my hind legs, sending my body hurdling into the wall next to us. Yelping, I shook my fur and righted myself, nodding a quick thanks in Griffin's direction.

From where I now stood, teeth bared and talons buried into the cold ground, I could watch most of the space without obstruction. To my left, wolves took on witch after witch, pairing up and circling each one much as they did with the prey they found in the forest. *I guess hunting isn't that bad after all.*

A low whine reached my ears and I perked them up, snapping my neck to face the sound. Near to me, another wolf had been hit. Its body dropped to the ground, front legs scraping the dirt before stilling. Above two other wolves, a flash of purple powder exploded, and they froze in their spots, falling to the side as the magic took control of their limbs.

We were losing numbers. Fast.

My snout raised upward, and I sniffed the air to find Billie, but instead, Victoria's face flashed before me. She stood at Catarina's side, each of them firing shot after shot of magic to push back the head witches on the outskirts of the catacombs. More rogue witches joined my pack in taking on the coven members closest to the circle.

We were making progress, but we weren't making it fast enough.

My sharpened teeth snapped and the muscles in my massive legs tensed while I scanned the catacombs for Billie. When I finally found her, a protective growl vibrated in my rib cage, and I pushed my way to get to her side. Another burst of purple powder flashed near me, and I skidded on the ground, changing direction to avoid it. It hit my tail and I cursed in my head as the damn thing fell lifeless at my back. The witch who got me cackled and I dove for her. Cutting through the air, I pushed her down, burying my front paws into her chest. She twisted under my weight, shoving her hands into her pockets in search of a crystal to use. She was too late.

My jaw unhinged and I threw myself at her neck, teeth piercing the soft skin. Her warm blood dripped down her neck and into my mouth. I tried not to swallow.

Tearing myself away, I pushed off the witch and towered over her body. Her hands clutched the wound at her throat, but it was pointless. I could see the life drain out of her as more blood poured from the wound.

Not wanting to witness her death, I twirled around and searched for Billie again.

If I could rub my eyes in wolf state, I would have done so.

Centered in the circle, Billie crouched over Logan's body with her hands stretched outward. She smiled and my stomach turned as her magic burst from her fingers and hit Theodora hard enough to send her flying backward. Billie's grin grew as she pulled stones from the ceiling to trample the high priestesses, and it immediately replaced the sick feeling in my stomach with pride. She had her magic back.

Kick their ass, babe!

As Billie stood, I tried to wiggle my limp tail with anticipation. She was so close. If she could take down the high priestesses, we'd be set. Now that she had magic, it shouldn't be that difficult for—

A blinding, scorching heat pummeled my heart and I yelped as it spread through me. My paws beat the ground, eyes scanning over the fur for fire. There was nothing there. At least, there were no flames. Instead, my chest shook and the skin beneath my gray fur glowed in changing colors. It was so beautiful, I almost forgot how fucking painful it was. Saliva dripped from my mouth and my eyes widened in shock as thin lines appeared beneath the surface of the fur. Glowing brightly, I could see them clear as day.

The lines swirled in intricate patterns, crawling up my body until they covered my chest and neck. My heart drummed and my breathing sped up as I watched the lines take over every part of me.

River?

Billie's voice called out and I drew my attention to her face, realizing she wasn't speaking at all. Her stunning features were a mixture of shock and happiness, and when I looked down, I saw the same lines on her body. An exact match.

I shook my head.

River, can you hear me?

Meeting her gaze, I howled loud enough to alert a few pack members, though no one left their post at the front lines.

What is happening? I swear she's talking.

I am, Billie's voice responded. *You can hear me, right?*

My head tilted. *What the actual fuck?*

Okay, we're going to need to discuss your language if this is going to be a thing now, hunter.

Unsure if I was going mental, I took a few steps back and dipped my snout down. In hungry whiffs, I attempted to sniff out magic residue I may have missed, but nothing was there. Whatever was going on wasn't the result of an attack so there was only one explanation for it. I jerked my head up, meeting Billie's sapphire eyes once more. *Are you in my head?* I thought as loud as I could.

Looks like it, Billie thought back, a slight smirk playing at her lips. *This is so freaking weird.*

What does this mean?

Billie looked to the lines covering even more of her body now, then to me. *Guess you were right about the lines, babe. I think we just got mated. Cool art, huh?*

I swore I could hear the wolf laugh in my head. This couldn't be real, could it? After all this time, the bond finally appeared and while I was deliriously happy to have it, it also scared me shitless. Though, being able to talk to Billie in my wolf form was pretty damn cool. And she was right. The art looked kickass.

My eyes met Billie's and I scraped a long nail across the floor. *What's our plan here? Please, tell me you have one.*

She grinned.

I sure do. Keep the head witches out of my way, I'm going

for the priestesses, Billie commanded. *Oh, I have my magic again. Like all of it.*

I smiled. Sort of. Hard to smile when you have a snout.

I know, babe. Now, go use it. Give those bitches hell.

Straightening, Billie rose over Logan's body. Her fingers wiggled, and as she stepped over the mind reaper to face the high priestesses, knots formed in the base of my gut. Her arms raised and her lips twitched, but she wasn't scared. Not even a little. I wasn't sure how I knew it, how I felt it, and yet, it was there just the same. Billie was hellishly pissed, and her emotions rolled through the catacombs, hitting me square in the chest. I let out a low whine, digging my talons deeper into the ground before forcing myself to move.

Billie had the priestesses covered, I was sure of it. Now, I had to uphold my end of the deal.

Canines out, I pushed back on my hind legs and galloped to join my pack. A middle-aged head witch slid into my peripheral vision, and I skidded to a stop, zeroing in on her frame. The heat of her body pulsed around her in the red glow I've become familiar with and as she turned toward me, I jumped.

Landing on her chest with my paws pressing her to the ground, I tore at her jugular. Blood poured, and this time, I felt no remorse. Everyone who dared get in my way would pay for it. Everyone would bleed.

A feral hunger blinded me, and I moved from witch to witch, my pack beside me. Around us, magic blasted, hitting wolves and witches alike. It couldn't stop us though. Couldn't even slow us down. The pack fed off my energy as we charged through the coven, and I fed off Billie's rising anger.

One by one, the head witches fell, screams parting their lips in agony.

A loud bang broke their cries, and I tore my jaw away from the witch I entrapped to look toward the circle. Awestruck, I watched as Billie's arms rose high above her. Shadows swarmed the space along her body and her legs shook as she pushed more of her magic into the catacombs. Several feet away from her, the high priestesses outstretched their hands to hold her off, though I noticed the strain in their eyes as they struggled to fight back. Sebyl's face dropped, and Billie sneered. Her fingers curled into fists, and she dropped to her knees, blasting magic into the ground and letting all hell break loose.

Chapter Thirty-eight

Billie

The power trapped inside my body wanted to be free, and I had no problem letting it escape. It had been so long since I've been able to use my magic, since I felt whole, that even an ounce of energy made my skin tingle. Except this wasn't an ounce at all. The magic flowed out of me in buckets, and the glimmering dots of light that signified its presence blinded me from seeing anything but what was right in front of me. Anything but my target.

Filling my lungs with air, I called for the spirit element in my blood and the shadows burst from my skin and surrounded me in their majestic darkness. They rushed over my body like a hurricane of fury and strength, and I fed off their energy, summoning the other elements to the surface. Deep down, the power of the elements crowded my chest, and when I pulled their combined magic into my fingers, my arms went numb. Sweat ran down my back as I raised my arms over my head and fisted my hands.

Before me, the high priestesses threw their magic in colorful rays at my shadows, trying to penetrate the wall I had erupted. Their futile blows crashed over my shield, doing nothing to weaken it.

Sebyl's face darkened and she let her putrid smile drop.

I got you now, asshole.

Calling on the elements, I dropped to my knees and punched my fists into the ground. My magic flowed into the earth, shaking the catacombs with so much force that the high priestesses' figures blurred before me.

The ground vibrated and cracks spread from my fists to their feet, making them topple backward to avoid falling through. Winds fast enough to tear down skyscrapers whipped around them, pushing the four women closer together. Above their heads, a massive storm cloud formed, and a booming thunder sounded only seconds before water rained down on them in waves.

I unclenched the fingers of my left hand and pressed it into the floor. Fire broke loose on my fingertips and I blew out a breath, sending it straight for Luna. The seer shrieked as blazing flames erupted over her long lace dress, and she dropped to the ground, rolling to put them out. Her hands reached for an amethyst, using its wind energy to blow out the fires and leaving behind torn fabrics and singed skin.

Next to her, Rhiamon thrust her sword in the air and sent it flying toward me. The blade pierced my shadows, the silver slicing through the magic with ease. Its tip glistened and I could see it barrel straight for my eyes.

Peeling one hand off the ground, I flicked my fingers and the sword changed direction, returning to its sender.

Rhiamon's eyes widened, and she attempted to move out of the way, but she was much too slow. The sword pierced her shoulder, sending her flying back and impaling her to the wall. She screamed in agony, and I grinned like a complete psycho.

Two down, two to go.

Returning my palm to the ground, I knelt and faced Theodora. The priestess was too busy throwing her pathetic fireballs to notice my attention burn into her. I closed my eyes, picturing the wind above her, and slammed it into her chest. Theodora dropped with a thud, gasps leaving her lips as she struggled against the air I forced into her lungs. She worked to keep her mouth sealed, but I pushed more of my magic out, using the wind to pry her lips open. When I had her squirming like the coward she was, I took it all back. Air rushed from her body, leaving her clutching her throat while I suffocated her. Theodora's eyes rolled back into her head, and she fell to the side, unconscious.

My gaze met Sebyl next.

The high priestess, the monster that raised me, trembled before me now. Her sad little magic that I once looked up to were parlor tricks to me now. I was so much stronger than her, stronger than all of them, and she damn well knew it.

Sebyl produced several more crystals, digging for their elements with a desperation that coated the air surrounding us. Unfortunately for her, the crystals would do nothing to hold me back. They certainly couldn't save her.

While the priestess worked to gather enough magic to attack me with, I turned inward. Reaching for the air element inside me, I wielded it to suit my needs. My body floated off the ground, feet scraping the earth, before the magic shot me up into the air. Legs dangling, I spread my arms wide and pulled on the stones lining the walls. I yanked them inward, thrusting the rocks at Sebyl with all my might.

She dodged a few, but a large stone tile knocked her in

the stomach and shot her to the side. The priestess fell to the ground, right next to her evil sisters.

As they huddled together, I considered letting them go. Only for a moment, of course. No matter how much I wished for things to have turned out differently, there was only one way to end this day.

The high priestesses had to die.

Pooling my magic into a massive ball, I threw my eyes open and floated closer to the priestesses. Their eyes bulged and their eyebrows raised as they watched me approach. I couldn't blame them, really. If I saw someone fly at me with a hurricane of shadows swirling the air and elemental magic on their fingertips, I'd have crapped my pants and run.

Except the priestesses did no such thing.

To my shock, they rose to stand on shaking legs and clutched their hands. The damn chanting they started earlier resumed and a bright blow glow formed around their bodies. "SHIT!" I yelled out. "They're trying to escape!"

My arms jerked forward, and I blasted the priestesses with all my power. Before I could hit them, an enormous portal opened and swallowed the women whole.

My head twisted to look back and my jaw hit the ground as a light tore from the portal to yank the head witches still breathing into the blue glow. Their bodies zoomed by me, one by one, disappearing from sight. When the last head witch vanished, the portal closed, leaving only a trail of blue magic behind.

I dropped hold of the elements, landing on the ground in the least flattering way possible. My butt hit the stone and I groaned as my hip bone cracked under my weight. The shadows crawled back into my body and the catacombs stopped shaking as I stilled the magic running through me.

Every freaking bone felt like someone had shattered it to pieces.

I hung my head into my chest and breathed shallow breaths, exhaustion taking me over.

Close to me, clamoring footsteps sounded, and when I looked up, River was towering over my frail body. His arms wrapped around me, scooping me up into a tight embrace, and I buried my face into his chest. The black lines that covered both our bodies pressed together and as his heart beat wildly in his chest, mine matched its rhythm.

I pulled back from him, gazing into the brilliant emeralds of his eyes, and a tear rolled down my cheek. He was okay. Thank the Goddess he was okay.

River smiled for a second before his lips crashed to mine and devoured me. Our tongues danced together, and each time I inhaled him, the burning in my chest intensified. *Damn, this bond thing will take some getting used to.*

No kidding, River thought to me.

I grimaced, tearing my lips from his. "Yeah, that's going to be a problem."

River's chest rumbled with a low laugh. "Don't want me hearing all your dirty thoughts, witch?" he teased. "'Cause I kind of like this."

"Of course you do, hunter," I bit back. "You're a control freak."

As River laughed again, I peered over his shoulder to scan the rest of the catacombs. The place looked as though a bomb went off in it, which I suppose was exactly what happened. Except it was me who went off. *Just damn fabulous.*

Wolves shifted back into their human form before my eyes, and I turned my gaze upward not to watch. Being a creep was not a great look, and I doubted anyone in the pack wanted me to see their privates. River certainly didn't. Even as I averted my gaze, I felt him shift his weight to turn us around so I'd look anywhere but at his shifting pack.

"Like I said," I whispered into his shoulder. "Total control freak."

He brushed his hand over my hair. "You're not hurt, right? I mean, whatever that shit was you just pulled looked mad powerful, but it didn't hurt you?"

I shook my head.

"Nope. I'm a little tired, but it's getting better by the second."

My racing mind settled, and my head cleared, making me instantly remember why we came to this horrid place in the first place. Turning to face the circle, I watched the rise and fall of our friends' chests as they lay on the cold ground, their arms and legs still strapped in place. We had to heal them fast before they lost any more blood.

Dropping my eyes to River's exposed body, I looked up at him and winked. "Maybe go cover up," I suggested. "I'm going to help Vic and the rogue witches heal everyone."

River nodded, reluctantly loosening his hold on me before leading his very naked pack out of the catacombs. He glanced back once before they disappeared and the heat in my chest returned tenfold.

Rubbing the pulsing lines on my chest, I turned to Vic, motioning for her to join me at the circle. When we reached our friends, Catarina and two rogue witches were already working their magic to heal Savannah, Logan, and Lorelei. I dropped next to Morgan while Vic took Mel's hands and fed her magic into a potion she rubbed on her skin. I was about to do the same when another body fell to the floor next to Morgan's head.

My heart broke when I let my gaze trail up Peyton's shaking body, landing on her face. Tears poured down her cheeks and she choked back sobs, unable to speak.

"I..." she whispered between cries. "She..."

Placing a hand on her shoulder, I squeezed it and forced out a smile. "It's okay. She'll be fine, I'll take care of her."

Peyton looked back to Morgan and ran a finger across her cheek.

"I can't believe I forgot her," she choked out. "I'm such an asshole."

"You're not," I said encouragingly. Turning to Vic, I pointed to her healing potion, and she tossed the vial my way without a second thought. I probably could have figured out a way to use my elemental magic to heal Morgan, but now was not the time to experiment. Rubbing the contents of the vial over Morgan's wounds, I connected to my magic and used the potion's power to trace the cuts. As the skin closed up, I let my attention focus on Peyton again. "The illusion spell the High Coven cast broke when they stopped casting the ritual. Everything should be back to normal now. None of this was your fault, Peyton," I said to her. "They spelled the entire town. There was nothing you could do. Morgan is back now, all of them are, and that's what we should focus on. She's been through Hell. She'll need you to be strong for her."

More tears ran down Peyton's face and she wiped them off with the sleeve of her sweatshirt. She took in a deep breath and cradled Morgan's head into her lap, lovingly brushing the reddish streaks of hair off the hunter's face. Peyton's bloodshot eyes snapped to me. "Thanks for not giving up on her," she said. Then gesturing to the others in the circle, "On any of them."

"That's what friends are—" I paused. "What family is for. You'd have done the same if the tables were reversed."

When Morgan's wounds healed, I wiped off the blood that dried around them and glanced over to our friends. They were still passed out, but the color began to return to their faces. My gaze flowed over Logan.

"When they feel better," I said to Peyton, "we need to figure out how Logan got spirit magic."

"Yeah, girl," my best friend said, stiffening. "That was a hella weird surprise for all of us."

Leaving her to stay with Morgan, I rose to stand and walked to Vic. "Thank you for your help. I'm seriously glad you found Catarina when you did. We'd be screwed without you guys."

Vic's inky gaze drifted from me to the rogue witches in the catacombs. The women worked together, gathering their dead and wounded, healing some while mourning the others. The entire place was covered in so much sadness, I could barely stand it. But I knew it wasn't for nothing. If the rogue witches didn't show up when they did, we wouldn't be standing here now. And we sure as hell wouldn't be healing our friends.

Despite the losses the High Coven handed us today, I knew it could have been worse. Though, that knowledge didn't do much to lessen the pain that tainted my heart in blackness.

"I'm sorry," I said in a hushed tone. "For all the women that died today."

Beside me, Vic cracked her knuckles and shoved her hands in her pant pockets. "We all knew what we were getting into," she said, surprising me with the strength in her voice. "Everyone here wants the High Coven defeated, not just you. Yes, we lost good witches today, we'll probably lose more before all of this ends, but it was necessary. The High Coven doesn't deserve the power they have, and they definitely don't deserve to have even more of it. We're going to stop them, Billie. I know we will."

"Okay," I said.

"So, wanna fill me in on that show you put on or not so much?"

Chuckling, I crossed my arms and nudged her side with my hip. "I will. I still don't even know what happened there, but I guess maybe-dad wasn't lying. The magic I felt, Vic, it wasn't anything I've known before. I wasn't controlling it. More like it was a part of me. Pretty freaky, if I'm being honest."

Vic's lips trembled. "Guess we're lucky you're on our side and not on theirs," she scoffed.

We stood in silence for a while, watching as everyone around us gathered their strengths again. The musty air of the catacombs filled my lungs and I let it simmer, locking the memory of the day deep into my brain so I would never forget what happened here. Every loss, every death, had to be remembered. It had to tear me apart until it melted into me. We may have stopped the coven today, but they would return. Worse, their power was growing, and I had no idea how or why. The high priestesses were willing to risk everything to open that portal, so much so they spelled an entire town to do so. Whatever waited on the other side was important to the coven, and I was going to find out what it was and stop them before they could succeed.

No big deal, right? Right.

Vic shuffled her feet and I ripped myself away from my thoughts to look at her.

"I'm going away for a little while," she announced. "With Catarina and the rogues. We'll work on finding out what we can about this mystery world the coven is obsessed with. But promise me if anything happens that you'll call? We'll work together on this."

"I will," I said. "Thank you. I have a feeling this will only get worse from here."

"HA!" Vic exclaimed. "Worse than a portal to some secret world, your weirdo magic, and finding out the reaper over there isn't just a regular shadower?"

I breathed out a laugh. "Yep. Probably worse than that. On the bright side, at least we know the coven doesn't have what it takes to open the portal. Yet. So that's something."

"Uh-huh…"

Looking around us, I nudged my head toward my passed out friends. "You guys should go," I said to my friend. "River and the pack will be back soon. We'll get everyone home safe. I doubt you want to be here when Mel wakes up and tears into Raiden for not remembering her."

Vic smiled, though the gesture felt uneasy and full of doubt. "Promise you'll call?"

"I swear on the Goddess."

As she turned to leave, I watched her and the rogue witches gather their sisters to head out. My heart grew heavy, and my gaze darkened, taking in my last exchange with Vic.

I glanced at Peyton, who was still hugging Morgan to her chest, and breathed out. At least we got them all back. And hey, I was officially mated to River. A pretty sweet turn around in the end.

My pulse slowed as I pressed a hand to my chest, letting the lines warm at my touch.

The High Coven may have gotten away, but that didn't mean they had us beat. If we could get through today, we could get through anything. As if in response, the lines vibrated under my skin, and a sense of relief washed over me. It wasn't mine. It was River's, but it felt just like my own. Our emotions and thoughts were tied with an invisible string now, and while that should have scared the crap out of me, it did quite the opposite.

We were stronger together.

Me, River, Peyton, Vic, the rogue witches. We were all tied together somehow and that was one thing the High Coven didn't have. Sure, they had their blind followers and their magic, but we had something else.

We had each other and that would help us take them down for good. No magic compared to the power I uncovered in Shadowhurst. Nothing matched family, not even the High Coven itself.

Chapter Thirty-nine

Billie

*B*y the time River drove me home from Tyler's funeral, my eyes were so puffy from crying, they were tiny slits on my face. The skin around them hurt to the touch from all the rubbing, and the knots in my stomach pushed nausea up my nose and throat. River parked the car behind Imala's SUV and ran around the side to open the passenger door for me. On any other day, I would have objected, but today, I needed all the help I could get.

So, I let him wrap an arm around me and drag me into the guesthouse, avoiding Thomas and Imala's concerned looks.

They had worn black, as we all did, and looking at them only reminded of Tyler. The nausea returned and I gaged into my mouth, bidding the two good bye as River tugged me away and into the confines of my room. From behind Thomas' shoulder, Silas cast an ominous look my way and his gold-rimmed glasses crept down his nose. No doubt the butler would sneak me food later, as he always did when I was upset. *Bless your perfect heart, Silas.*

By the time we reached my bedroom, my legs were mush and my eyes drooped with a heavy need to sleep. River poured me into the bed, tucking covers over my weak body before taking off his shoes to lie beside me. His heavy arms folded around me, pressing my neck into his chest. As his breaths vibrated at my back, my lips tightened and I closed my eyes, letting sleep take me.

An unfamiliar melody drifted over me, and my eyes flew open. Around me, thick foliage unfolded, covering every inch of the foreign land I stood in. Flowers in colors my brain couldn't comprehend lined the trees and thick vines crawled over every branch, drooping down like green tears.

The wind rustled the trees and brilliant puffs of purple fell from their leaves, covering my head. I gasped as the sense of magic drifted through me.

My hands trembled, and when I looked down at them, my jaw slacked. The air glowed a beautiful pink hue. No, wait, that wasn't right. It wasn't the air that was glowing. It was me.

Letting out another surprised gasp, I tried to shake the pink away, but it stayed glued to my skin. Grimacing, I pushed aside a low-hanging vine and stepped through, my feet floating to bring me forward.

More of the strange forest unfolded before me, and I could hear trickling water near to where I stood. I followed the sound, cutting through the foliage and letting the magic of the forest permeate my body as I walked. When I reached the water, my eyes widened.

In front of me, a breathtaking waterfall the color of raspberries crashed into an opal-hued river, I dropped to my knees, running a palm over the water's surface. Sparkles of magic drifted up to my hand, and I yanked it out before they reached me. The water rippled, waves parting the surface to reveal an image of a world I knew like the rear of my hand. Shadowhurst.

Blood stained the streets and magic rushed the air as the image came into focus. Acid and horror rose in my throat as I watched witches fight against an opponent just barely out of sight. In the front lines, Vic and Catarina took the lead, blasting magic from the crystals clutched in their fingers. Their magic exploded, and the water rippled again, bringing more of Shadowhurst into focus.

My arms slacked and my body froze as I watched the image reform to show me more of the town. Fires burned as high as the sky. Houses and buildings engulfed in their destruction. A burst of magic carried through the streets, colliding with something with a bang. My eyes narrowed on the object, realizing too late that it was a massive sword. At its hilt, rough fingers tightened, and I followed the arm connected to them.

A horrified yelp escaped me when the face of a man met my gaze. His deep-set blue marine eyes tightened into thin lines as he flipped the sword around and sent it flying toward the source of the magic. Toward my friends.

"What is this?" I asked the water, but it only rippled in response. The waves flowed outward, giving me a better view of the man and the army flanking his side.

Behind them, large wooden constructs obscured the horizon, and spit collected in my mouth when I understood what they were.

More stakes than I could count lined the streets of Shadowhurst, each one obscured by flames. My stomach turned as I focused my eyes on them. Tied to the stakes and burning into oblivion were witches. I couldn't see their faces, but I could feel their pain even through the water.

My kind was burning, again. The hunters found us. They found us all.

I woke up in a cold sweat, screaming and shaking. Actually, I wasn't shaking. Someone else was doing it for me. My eyes fluttered open to find myself upright on the edge of my bed with River's powerful grip on my shoulders. My body rumbled as he continued to shake me awake, panic on his face. "Babe! Babe, you're having a bad dream. Wake up!"

I pushed back on his chest, forcing him to stop. A migraine reared its ugly head in the back of my eyes, and I rubbed at them, wincing from the friction the motion left on my irritated skin.

"Geez! Enough!" I bit out. "I'm awake. Goddess, you're going to make my head fall off if you keep doing that."

"Sorry," River said. "You were screaming and I couldn't get you to snap out of it."

"I had a nightmare. All good now."

"What the hell did you see to make you scream like that?" River asked just as his phone vibrated on the nightstand. He held up a finger, letting me know to hold that thought, and answered. "Sav?"

I tried to hear what Savannah was saying on the other line, but she was too quiet.

"What do you mean other hunters?" River asked. "When? Where?"

I sat in silence, watching the color leave River's face while he listened. Our bond beat against my chest and his intense emotions rolled around inside me. When River hung up the phone, his tan skin was the color of ash.

"What was that about?" I asked.

River's head shook and I could feel his confusion through our bond. "That was Sav. She said something weird. I don't even understand it."

"What did she say?"

"That there are other hunters. Witch hunters. They contacted her and the others after the funeral, asking to meet the hunter faction of Shadowhurst. She didn't believe them at first, but they said some shit that only hunters would know. Details of our families, our training, everything we learned in those stupid books at the library. She doesn't know how many there are, but..."

Frustrated, I tucked a finger under his chin and brought his face up to meet my gaze. "But what?"

River swallowed hard. "They're coming here. To Shadowhurst. They followed the coven here and now, they're on their way to town."

"WHAT?!? WHY?!?" I yelled. Not my finest moment.

River frowned. "They're after every witch they can find, and they want our help."

Bright lights danced in my vision and my knees knocked against each other. Images of burning stakes flashed before me, and alarm gripped me in a vice. The scent of the witch graveyard filled my nostrils as I leaned back against the pillow and took a ragged breath in.

Hunters. Witches. Burning stakes.

History was about to repeat itself in this little town built on murder and injustice. Something new was coming to

Shadowhurst, and this time, it would take more than my shadows and a few spells to stop it. This threat wasn't one I could fix with magic. It differed from anything I understood.

This was a threat steeped in history, and it would take history to stop it.

Turns out, no matter how deep you hide those skeletons in the closet, they always crawl right back out. They are, after all, only bone and hatred. Two things that burrow deep down and infest everything in their path.

That was what was coming for us now. Bones, hatred, and a whole lot of unearthed bullshit.

Somehow, I had the feeling that whatever was going to happen next would make the High Coven look like child's play.

Wrapping my fingers around River's, I pressed my fore-head to his and closed my eyes. *Better get ready, hunter,* I thought into our bond. *Things are about to get bloody.*

Ready to dive into the next mystery to hit Shadowhurst? Witch hunters are coming to town. If you thought the High Coven was bad, you'll love to hate these guys. Armed to the teeth and full of ill intentions, the hunters are dead-set on, well, death. Will Billie be able to lead them away from her friends or will this be the task that breaks our young witch? Find out in Book Five of the Shadowhurst Mysteries: **Mirror of Secrets**. CLICK HERE to read **Mirror of Secrets** now!

You can also check out the cover and description for the Mirror of Secrets below.

Brutal witch killers are coming to town, and guess who they can't wait to see?

I don't want to brag, but I'm pretty good at fooling people, but even my charm can't save me or my witch friends from these guys.

A new plan is in order. I only wish I knew what that plan was.

The witch hunters know what they want—the High Coven. It's up to me to make sure they don't get anywhere near them. All I have to do is stay under the radar and try not to get killed.

Simple, right?

Not even close.

Let's just hope I make it out alive.

CLICK HERE to start reading the **Mirror of Secrets** now!

Haven't read the beginning of the story and wondering what's going on? **Witch of Shadows** will catch you right up! Read the first book of the Shadowhurst Mysteries here:

READ THE BOOK NOW!

Interested in finding out what happened to Beatrix Stonewall? Read the prequel novella Coven of Deception for FREE!

READ COVEN OF DECEPTION

Magic is real and it's coming for you.
Did you know all those fairytales you heard as a kid

about witches weren't fairytales at all? Well, neither did I. Imagine my surprise when I found out that not only did I possess magic, but that an entire secret coven of witches lurked right under my nose my whole life.

When my powers first manifested, I wanted nothing to do with them, but as I discovered more of the women welcoming me into their fold, I couldn't get enough! Unfortunately, life has a tendency of knowing when you're happy and jumps at the chance to throw a wrench in all your plans.

That's exactly what happened to me. One minute I'm starting a new life and minding my own business, and the next, I'm barreling face first into trouble. Oh, did I mention the mysterious, alluring stranger that won't leave me alone no matter how much I push him away?

So, yeah. I think it's safe to say I'm in for quite the ride. Care to join me?

Just kidding. Stay away if you know what's good for you.

Start reading Coven of Deception by CLICKING HERE.

ACKNOWLEDGMENTS

Shadowhurst just keeps getting creepier and creepier! I cannot begin to describe how much I loved writing this book. As the mystery of the town unfolds, I get more excited with each word written and while this book had some challenges, I am unbelievably proud of how it turned out.

An immense amount of love and gratitude goes to my wonderful partner for his continuous ability to put up with me when I am in the middle of a book. He's honestly my biggest supporter and I love him for it!

To my parents, thank you for letting me bounce ideas off you and the wonderful and creative advice you've given me to make this book so much better.

Tremendous gratitude to my beta readers and critique partners for your honest feedback on the earlier drafts of this book. You help me get out of my head and behind the story, in ways I couldn't imagine on my own.

And as always, to my readers. You are my rock and I love each one of you like family.

Keep fighting for your magic!

ABOUT THE AUTHOR

A.N. Sage has spent most of her life waiting to meet a witch, vampire, or at least get haunted by a ghost. In between failed seances and many questionable outfit choices, she has developed a keen eye for the extra-ordinary.

Since chasing the supernatural does not pay the bills, she dabbled in creative entrepreneurship, marketing and retail management. A.N. spends her free time reading and binge-watching television shows in her pajamas.

Currently, she resides in Toronto, Canada with her husband who is not a creature of the night.

A.N. Sage is a Scorpio and a massive advocate of leggings for pants.

For more books and updates:
www.ansage.ca

Connect on social media:
Facebook Group:
facebook.com/groups/945090619339423/
Instagram:
instagram.com/a.n.sage/
Twitter:
twitter.com/ANsageWrites
Facebook:

facebook.com/ansagewrites

Pinterest:

pinterest.ca/ansagewrites

Goodreads:

goodreads.com/author/show/18901100.Alexis_N_Sage

Amazon:

amazon.com/author/a.n.sage